"Now tell me what I can expect from this initial hearing. I see it's set in six weeks."

"The key to all of this is Kristi must show proof that you are mentally incompetent. At the hearing, the judge will review the case and decide whether to throw it out or order a complete psychiatric evaluation."

"And if he does order an evaluation, who pays for it?" Paula felt her anger swell again.

"She does. Now, since you purchased the bed-and-breakfast, have you had any dealings that might lead the judge to question your mental stability?"

Paula piqued at the question. "Absolutely not!"

James smiled. "I have to ask these questions, Paula. It's better you tell me today than for me to be surprised in court."

"I'm sorry," Paula said. "This whole thing has me angry and hurt. In answer to your question, I can't recall a single incident in which I did not use proper judgment."

"Are there any new relationships?"

Paula sat straight up in the chair. "You mean a gentleman friend?" she asked incredulously. The wheels began to turn in her mind.

"Yes, that is what I'm asking. Are you seeing anyone who Kristi would definitely find as a threat to your financial security?"

Paula hesitated. Like a puzzle, it all began to make sense. "Yes, I have a friend. He's the contractor who did all the work for me. We've become very close."

He lifted a fresh sheet of paper and raised his pen to write. "Tell me about this fellow. What has Kristi seen of him, and why might she consider him a threat?"

DIANN MILLS lives in Houston, Texas, with her husband Dean. They have four grown sons. She wrote from the time she could hold a pencil, but not seriously until God made it clear that she should write for Him. After three years of serious writing, her first book, *Rehoboth*, won favorite Heartsong Presents historical for 1998. Other publishing credits include magazine articles and short stories, devotionals, poetry, and internal writing for her church. She is an active church choir member and a church librarian.

Books by DiAnn Mills

HEARTSONG PRESENTS
HP191—Rehoboth

Don't miss out on any of our super romances. Write to us at the following address for information on our newest releases and club information.

Heartsong Presents Readers' Service
PO Box 719
Uhrichsville, OH 44683

Country
Charm

DiAnn Mills

Heartsong Presents

This book is a dedicated to my mother Betty Barett, Charlene Mills, and Beatrice Vergne. All my love!

A note from the author:
I love to hear from my readers! You may correspond with me by writing: **DiAnn Mills**
Author Relations
PO Box 719
Uhrichsville, OH 44683

ISBN 1-57748-547-5

COUNTRY CHARM

Cover illustration by Kathy Arbuckle.

PRINTED IN THE U.S.A.

one

"Really, Mother, you've got to be kidding. This place is a dump!" Kristi Franklin exclaimed with a toss of her head.

Paula Franklin ignored her daughter and clicked the camera. "Oh, I don't think so at all. In fact, this big old farmhouse has charm."

"Charm? You can't possibly be considering sinking money into this thing," Kristi said, running her fingers through shoulder-length, cocoa brown hair. "Daddy would roll over in his grave, if he knew your ridiculous plans. The roof needs repair, the dilapidated front porch looks dangerous, and the paint is chipped so badly that you can't tell the color of the house."

Paula smiled and viewed the frustration in her daughter's face.

"Mother, listen to me. You can live quite well on Daddy's insurance money. Why risk losing it with a renovation project like this? For that matter, why do you need all the headaches of a bed-and-breakfast?"

Paula bent in the tall grass to snap another picture. Stepping closer, she took a shot of the sagging front porch. Another click captured the broken wooden steps and rotting floor where pink and purple spring wildflowers peeked through.

"Mother, be careful. There are probably snakes in there," Kristi warned, impatience clipping every word.

"I'm wearing boots," Paula replied.

"Not on the seat of your pants," Kristi pointed out.

Slowly Paula stood and faced her daughter. "I've got lots of pictures to take. Do you want to keep me company or continue to complain?" She peered deep into Kristi's troubled face.

"I'm not complaining. I just want you to see what a ludicrous venture this is."

Paula shook her head and grinned. "Some people my age

go through a midlife crisis. I prefer to go through a midlife adventure."

"But with Daddy's money?" Kristi protested.

"And what would you rather I do with the insurance money?" Paula asked quietly.

"Invest it," Kristi instantly replied.

"Ah, I see. And you would be my personal stockbroker?"

"Mother, please. Investing Daddy's money into some good, secure divested funds makes more sense than throwing it into a paint can and a keg of nails."

"Correction, Kristi. It is not Daddy's money; it is mine. I've thought and prayed about this for a long time. I am buying this big old farmhouse. In fact I have three bids on the work needed to make it a bed-and-breakfast." Paula paused, wishing her daughter understood her plans. "Please, honey. This is a dream your father and I shared. We wanted a big place like this to open a Christian bed-and-breakfast. My mind is set, and I really would like for you to accept my decision."

Kristi sighed heavily and crossed her arms in a stubborn stance. "Accept, yes; agree, never. You can live here if you want, Mother, but I prefer to live in Austin."

"Suit yourself," Paula said, heading to the side of the house. "Are you coming while I take more pictures?"

"I suppose," Kristi grumbled, trailing after her. "It's probably overrun with rattlers and roaches."

Paula disregarded the last statement and snapped picture after picture of the house, making sure to capture all the angles, including missing roof shingles and cracked windows. She felt elated. A spark of enthusiasm missing from the past five years since John's heart attack took his life sent her imagination soaring. It had been too long since a project burned through her veins like this one did.

In the beginning, she thought a bed-and-breakfast would be a way to keep John's memory alive, a tribute to their twenty-five years together. The more she considered the project, the more she realized its worth in healing her grief. Paula knew she could sink her teeth into this endeavor and with God's help make it work! After all, she'd researched, visited, and planned it for several years.

The eighteen-room, one-hundred-year-old white farmhouse setting near Brenham, Texas, held all of the characteristics of a delightful bed-and-breakfast. A solid foundation, large rooms, lots of wood, three working brick fireplaces, plus an assortment of antiques ready for restoration appealed to her taste and sense of adventure. The farmhouse with its chipped paint and obvious repairs seemed to be an answer to prayer; and best of all, the price fit her budget.

She took a sideways glance at her daughter. At twenty-four, Kristi had moved up the corporate ladder of a brokerage firm through the glass ceiling to a position of respect. Dark-eyed and pretty, she mirrored her father, but only in looks. John Franklin never believed power and prestige produced happiness, quite the contrary. He knew his joy came from the Lord, and together he and Paula had brought up Kristi with the same ideals. Somewhere along the way, their daughter chose a different path.

"Does this place have any acreage?" Kristi asked, shading her eyes and looking toward a grove of trees.

"Yes, there are fifteen acres, which include producing pecan trees."

Kristi rolled her eyes. "So when you aren't playing maid and cook to the guests, you can pick up pecans?"

Paula smiled. "Exactly, and even more exciting than the grove is a narrow winding stream that runs through the rear of the property."

"Oh, great. Now you're going to dig worms and fish!"

"Maybe," Paula replied thoughtfully. "A fishing hole hadn't occurred to me. Say, what about a tour of the inside?"

"Is it safe?"

Paula couldn't help but laugh. "Of course it is." She stood and allowed a light breeze to blow through her hair. She breathed in deeply, taking in the fragrance of distant honeysuckle. "I love this place," she murmured.

"I can tell you do," Kristi said gently. "But Mother, you are forty-nine years old. Why don't you let me invest your money and take it easy? If you feel the urge to do something, then volunteer more at your church."

Paula shook her head sadly. "You truly don't understand. I don't want to sit back in an easy chair and play bridge or spend hours each week lunching with lady friends. Your father lived every moment to its fullest, and I want to do the same. God gave me a life with talents, and He intends for me to use them. I firmly believe God wants me to turn this old house into a Christian bed-and-breakfast to glorify Him. Be happy with me. Dream a little and relax."

Paula saw her stiffen, and she met her daughter's eyes with a silent challenge. A real battle stood ready, but Kristi said nothing. Letting the camera dangle from around her neck, Paula reached out to take her hand.

"Come on, let me give you a tour. It's a beautiful home."

ช้

"So, how many bedrooms are there?" Kristi asked as she descended the stairs.

"Six up and one down," Paula answered. "The long, rather narrow room upstairs would make a beautiful sitting room. Of course bathrooms have to be added and most likely the wiring needs updating."

"What about all of the rooms downstairs?"

"Umm," Paula said dreamily. "I envision antiques, flowers, a library, and a music room. Lots of Texas memorabilia—"

"Hello?" a male voice called from the front entrance. "Hello?"

"Yes, we're coming downstairs," Paula replied. She hurried down the stairs to the foyer, where a man dressed in jeans and a blue denim shirt awaited them.

"Mrs. Franklin?" he asked hesitantly, as he removed a tan colored cowboy hat.

Paula nodded. "Yes, can I help you?" She noticed his deep brown lizard boots and western belt buckle.

He stuck out his hand to shake hers. "I'm Rick Davenport, a local contractor. I heard you're buying this place and are taking bids on remodeling it for a bed-and-breakfast. Your realtor told me I'd probably find you here."

Paula smiled. "It's a pleasure to meet you, Mr. Davenport. I've already solicited three bids from other contractors, but you are welcome to make one also. Oh, pardon me, this is my daughter, Kristi."

"Good to meet you both," Rick said heartily, and his crystal blue eyes sparkled. "This was my grandmother's home, and I've got a lot of fond memories of this place. Remodeling and restoring homes isn't my usual line of work. I normally stick to new constructions, but this would be a mighty fine project. I'd thought about buying it myself, but it's so big that I didn't know what I'd do with it."

Paula dug inside of her purse and produced a folded sheet of paper. "Here, Mr. Davenport. This is a rough idea of what I need, and I realize you will have to draw up specs and such. My realtor has the key and you can make an appointment with him."

"Thank you, ma'am, I'd be honored to make a bid for you." Rick shook his head and looked around the foyer. "Gracious, I remember a lot of good times here. My grandmother was a jewel; she had more spirit than a frisky colt, and she needed it with six boys and five girls."

"I bet you could tell me a lot of stories," Paula commented.

"You bet. Grandma had a ton of grandkids, and what one of us didn't think of to get into trouble, the other one did." Rick grinned and Paula noticed his deeply tanned skin and thick silver hair. "Here's my card," he said.

"And here's my name and address." Paula pulled a small scratch pad from her purse and handed it to him with a smile.

"I'll look forward to visiting with you about this," Rick said. "May I ask you something?"

"Certainly."

"Are you wanting to tear down walls and start all over?"

"Oh, no. I want to keep everything as is, except for the addition of bathrooms and updating the kitchen. One thing for sure, I need to strip all of this wood. It's much too beautiful to be painted."

Rick smiled genuinely. "I'll be sure to include that in my bid, and thank you for your time. It's been a pleasure talking to you and your daughter."

Paula closed the door behind Rick Davenport and turned to Kristi. "Wasn't he a nice man?"

Kristi rolled her eyes. "He looked like he just stepped off the rodeo line. Mother, you watch him. He looks like a gold digger to me."

Paula shook her head. It did little good to argue with her daughter when she stood square in the middle of one of her authoritative moods.

❧

Two weeks passed, and the realtor pressured Paula to close on the deal, but she knew the bids on the house were crucial in making her decision.

"Without those bids, I cannot and will not purchase the property, Mr. Snyder," Paula explained. "Surely you understand this is a business venture, and without an estimate on the necessary work, I am in the dark as to how much money I'll need to fix it up."

"Understandable, Mrs. Franklin. Do you mind if I contact the gentlemen preparing the bids?" Tim Snyder asked.

"By all means. I'm as anxious as you are." Paula hung up the phone. She had the funds to close on the property with plenty left for the work, but John had taught her to be frugal and firm in matters dealing with money.

Two days later the realtor called. He had secured all four bids for her inspection. "Can you meet with me tomorrow morning? I've got four sets of plans for you to see."

"Great. I'll drive out and plan to spend the day. Will the gentlemen be available for questions?"

"Yes, ma'am," he replied, "and I have their pager numbers."

Paula felt like a child looking forward to Christmas. She loved that big old farmhouse and had wanted it for her own since she first saw it. Between the huge oak in the front yard and the porch winding around to the south side of the home, Paula considered it sold. She envisioned huge ferns hanging from the porch and several rocking chairs filled with guests sipping gourmet coffee in the morning and fresh squeezed lemonade during the evening. Amidst a flowerbed of red roses, a sign out front would read: The Country Charm, A Christian Bed-and-Breakfast.

In the rear, she envisioned a white gazebo with the faint sounds of piped-in music, most likely a dulcimer playing old hymns. In the summer she'd host buggy rides, and in the fall and winter, hayrides. *Oh my,* she thought, *every holiday will be more wonderful than the last.* Paula imagined showers, weddings, birthdays, and reunions—all of them special at The Country Charm. Naturally, she'd have plenty of food, coffee, tea, and lemonade for everyone.

John told her once that she had the gift of hospitality, and she always had more fun than her guests did. *Oh Lord, You and I will have a wonderful time with this bed-and-breakfast. Thank You for the opportunity to glorify You in all the work ahead.*

৯

Paula rolled the final set of specs back together and secured them with a rubber band. She'd taken over two hours to examine each bid and proposed plan. Gathering them up, she proceeded into the realtor's office.

"Can I take these out to the house?" Paula asked. "I'd like to sit down with them there to make my final decision."

"I don't see why not," Tim Snyder replied. "How do they look to you?"

"Well, one is rather high. Two others are real close, and the fourth bid is very attractive," Paula said thoughtfully.

"Which one is the lowest?"

"Rick Davenport's," she replied simply. "What can you tell me about his company?"

Tim scooted back his chair and folded his hands across his lap. "Frankly, I'm surprised Rick's bid came in low. He's an excellent contractor, but he usually focuses his work on huge homes, more of the estate type. I don't know why he's even interested in the place."

"He told me it was his grandmother's home," Paula offered, pulling out the Davenport set of plans. "I met him one afternoon when he stopped at the house."

"Ah, now I understand his interest," Tim replied with a nod.

Paula took a deep breath and tucked her hair behind her ear as she considered her next words. "I think we can work out things today, but I would like to possibly meet Mr. Davenport at the property. If all goes well, then I'll make an offer."

"I'll make the arrangements," he said with a smile.

"How long will it take for possession, providing this is a cash deal?" Paula asked, yearning to bring the last several weeks of negotiations to a close.

"Won't take long at all," Tim eagerly replied. "Most likely you can take possession at closing."

two

"So, Mr. Davenport, why is your bid lower when you plan to use a better grade of materials, including the electrical wiring and plumbing, and I see you plan to assist me in stripping the woodwork?" Paula asked, as she and Rick walked around the outside of the farmhouse. She noticed he wasn't much taller than her five feet nine inches. Then again, she thought of herself as too tall for a woman.

"Simple," Rick said with a chuckle. "I don't plan to make any money on this deal." He stopped to examine a piece of rotting board on the back porch.

Paula eyed him curiously, if not suspiciously. "Why? Aren't you in business to make a profit?"

"Well, not on this project. Remember my grandmother lived in this house, and my dad grew up here. What you want to do preserves their memory. I only wish I had the time and creativity to do the same thing."

"Are you proposing a partnership?" she asked with a hint of teasing.

"No, ma'am. This is all yours," he replied with a smile. "Truthfully I admire your plans, and I'd be honored to do the work."

"Then the bid is yours," Paul stated, certain Rick Davenport would perform an excellent job. "I'll have my attorney draw up a check for the realtor and the advance for you."

The eighty-mile drive back to Austin flew by as Paula realized her dream was taking hold. She wanted to move in right away, but Rick explained some crucial work must be completed before living arrangements would be suitable and safe.

Once back at home, she considered the mound of pictures and ideas spread across her dining room table—over a decade of keepsakes torn from magazines and brochures of other bed-and-breakfasts. An antique trunk set full of old quilts, doilies, dresser scarves, pieces of lace, and antique jewelry ready to be artfully placed in The Country Charm. A nearby storage building held precious old pieces of furniture, dishes, glassware, and various other items including a weathervane and a goat cart. The antiques were an inheritance from John's mother, and she couldn't wait to use them.

Did she dare tell Kristi? No doubt her daughter would be horrified of her decision. Paula remembered their last words were less than pleasant.

"You'll regret squandering Daddy's money," Kristi warned during a phone conversation earlier that morning. "I assure you my attorney will examine your dealings inside and out."

Paula felt a surge of blood rise to her face. Normally she ignored her daughter's bossy attitude, but this time her words bordered upon a threat. "Your attorney will not have access to my actions," she said firmly. "I have my own attorney and accountant, both of whom are quite capable of advising me on my legal and financial matters."

"But that farmhouse is not where you should place Daddy's money," Kristi insisted, her voice rising. Paula heard a heavy sigh. "This conversation is pointless until you come to your senses."

Paula remembered the click of the receiver and realized her daughter had hung up the phone. *Lord, what happened to my sweet Kristi? She has no respect for anything I say or do. When did she grow so bitter?*

Paula understood her daughter still mourned her father's death. She'd been cool and aloof since John died. Kristi stated she didn't need counseling, God, or her old friends. She had crept into a hard-shell cocoon and isolated herself from displaying any emotions. Luckily she finished college and obtained a master's degree in business administration, and she now worked on her doctorate while at a full-time job. Kristi had no time for anything except that which would further her career.

Paula took a deep breath and decided to keep her dealings to herself. No point agitating Kristi if she didn't have to. Except she had to tell someone about the farmhouse before she burst! She dialed the phone and listened to it ring three times before an answering machine picked up.

"Hey, Barbara, this is Paula. I bought the farmhouse! I'm so excited. Call me so we can set a time for you to go see my new investment."

"Hold on, I'm here," Barbara said, picking up the phone. "I was heading out when I heard your voice. So you got the house?"

"I sure did. When do you want to see it? I mean, do you want to see it?"

"Yes, and Saturday morning," Barbara replied excitedly. "Oh, I can't wait."

"Oh, you'll love it, and Saturday sounds great. I'm supposed to meet the contractor then, too," Paula said. "Can we leave as early as eight? We can stop for coffee and bagels on the way out of town."

"I'll be ready," Barbara assured her.

Barbara Patrick, a petite brown-eyed blond, had been Paula's best friend since college days. They'd been quite a team, especially with Paula's height, hazel eyes, and auburn hair. From sorority sisters to sisters in Christ, the two had weathered child-rearing, laughter, tears, college expenses, and now the fight with middle-age spread. Barbara and her husband, Wade, had stood right beside her through John's tragic heart attack and the horrible grief following the funeral. Paula didn't know what she would have done without them.

❧

Saturday morning, the two women rushed through bagels and coffee and headed for Brenham. Paula had loaded her sport utility vehicle with wallpaper books, flooring samples, and bits of fabric. She realized decorating plans were premature, but in the excitement, she felt compelled to hurry things along.

"Are you planning to hang all of the paper yourself?" Barbara asked, lifting a wallpaper book from the seat behind her.

"I think so. After all, I've done it for years. Do you remember the first time we hung paper together?" Paula asked with a laugh.

"Kristi's nursery," chimed in Barbara. "We looked like an old Lucy and Ethel episode. I kept trying to show you how to hang the paper, except you stood a head taller and it kept falling down."

"I miss those days," Paula said wistfully. "Kristi was much easier to handle then."

Barbara frowned. "Is she being a pill again?"

"Oh yes. She hates the idea of my bed-and-breakfast, but I can't go through life trying to please her."

"Did you explain this dream originated with her father?" Barbara asked gently.

"Sure did, and I also explained how I had prayed about it. However. . .oh, let's not talk about gloomy things. Barb, I have markers in that wallpaper book. Tell me what you think."

ॐ

"I love it!" Barbara squealed, bounding up the stairs like a teenager. "Paula, this will be so much fun. How ever did you find this place?"

"By taking a drive through the country after spending a night at a bed-and-breakfast in Brenham," Paula explained, rushing up the stairs behind her. "Really, I just drove by and saw the for-sale sign.

After a tour, the two ended up in the kitchen examining every nook and cranny. An old oak table and three chairs, one with a broken leg, caught Barbara's attention. She scrutinized it carefully, then her eyes moved around the room.

"Tell me, what do you plan to do in here?" Barbara asked, stooping to examine a cast-iron cooking stove in the corner. She wiped off some dirt with her finger, then rubbed harder with a tissue. "How in the world did those ladies cook with these things? I wonder how much wood they used for fried chicken or biscuits."

"I imagine it took years of practice," Paula said, thoughtfully looking around her. "This kitchen desperately needs updating so I can use it efficiently. I'm thinking of replacing the cracked vinyl floor with a wooden one, probably oak. You know, I bet there is a wood floor beneath it. Then I'd like cabinets in a deep country red with a forest green granite-type countertop."

"Good, keep going," Barbara urged. "You have always been the creative one."

"Right," Paula laughed. "I'm not creative, just brave. Well, I'm leaning toward a huge, green-checked wallpaper and a sunflower border picking up the green and red. That's all I have for now except to add some roosters for accent. And the cast iron stove will be a conversation piece with ivy and other added touches. Do you think it sounds bizarre?"

"No, it sounds perfect. It's all you," Barbara insisted, waving her arms in a most dramatic way. "Hey, someone just pulled up in a white truck," she announced, standing on her tiptoes to see through the dirt-smudged window. "Looks like one of those new models, too."

"Oh, it's the contractor," Paula replied, taking her own look. "Wonderful. He has the specs with him."

Barbara continued to stare out the window at Rick Davenport. "Say, he's good-looking, Paula."

She looked at her friend oddly. "I hadn't noticed, but he is friendly."

"Um, is he wearing a wedding ring?" Barbara asked barely above a whisper. "I wish this window wasn't so filthy."

"Barbara, for heaven's sake," Paula said, embarrassed with her friend's comment.

"I'm only looking out for you, but truthfully I can't see much of anything."

"Oh, stop gawking at the window!" Paula ordered through a whisper. "I'm not interested—not in him or anyone else. I've got enough problems without complicating life with a man."

"A man doesn't complicate your life, Paula; he complements it," Barbara pointed out, with a teasing air.

Paula shook her head and crossed her arms. "I had the best husband in the world, and God took him home. I don't want another one."

Moments later, Rick knocked at the door, but before Paula answered it, she gave Barbara a silent threat. "Don't you dare say a word," she mouthed.

"I promise," Barbara whispered, her brown eyes dancing, and broke into a girlish giggle.

❧

Paula labored over the architectural drawings before her. She mentally pictured the new electrical wiring and where outlets and lighting fixtures would be placed in each room.

"Okay," she said with a determined nod. "I think I understand this electrical business. Now could you explain the plumbing?"

Rick smiled, his crystal blue eyes twinkling. "Of course." He pointed to the upstairs area on the specs. "Each bedroom will have its own bath, except for the two bedrooms on the end. Those two rooms are already connected, so possibly sharing a bath won't be a problem. The other four bedrooms are large and the plumbing coming up the walls will allow a separate bath on each side without interfering with the closets. Do you follow me, Mrs. Franklin?"

"Yes, this is easier than the electrical stuff, and please call me Paula."

He grinned. "Thank you, and feel free to call me Rick. I should have brought some coffee for us. I apologize for not thinking about it."

"Oh, I'm not doing a thing," Barbara said. "I can run into Brenham and pick up some coffee, and by the looks of things, I'd better bring lunch."

Rick stood and pulled his wallet from his jeans pocket. "The least I can do is buy lunch." He handed Barbara two bills, and she thanked him before tucking them into her purse. After jotting down their orders and getting instructions for a good restaurant, Barbara drove off in Paula's car.

"She is a very nice lady," Rick said with a lazy drawl.

Suddenly Paula felt painfully aware of being alone with him. "Yes, Barbara and I have been friends forever. I don't know what I would do without her."

"I think God gives us friends to remind us of Him," Rick said, sitting again at the old oak table.

"So you're a Christian?" Paula asked with a smile.

"Yes, ma'am. A person couldn't be around my grandmother and my dad very long and not accept the Gospel."

"Good, perhaps now you understand how I feel about God calling me to open this bed-and-breakfast." Paula couldn't stop smiling. She felt so pleased that the man who would be in charge of making necessary renovations also knew the Lord.

Rick shook his head and laughed heartily.

He does have a most pleasant laugh, she thought decisively. It seemed to start from his toes and work its way up.

"Ma'am, I believe I'd have done this work for free, well almost for free. I'm still a businessman."

"I'm really glad we're working together," Paula said honestly. "I have such a peace about our business relationship."

"We'll see how you feel after I finish going over the plumbing. I've never explained wiring and plumbing to a woman before, but I'll do my best."

For the next hour, Rick pointed out where every major kitchen appliance would need to fit and necessary plumbing to accommodate Paula's plans.

"What did your grandmother use this room for?" Paula asked, standing and stretching her long legs and pointing to a room with an outside entrance.

Rick stood with her and peered inside. "In the beginning, she used it as a porch, then later my granddad closed it in, and she stored all of her canned goods there." He walked to the far end of the kitchen. "This old screened-in porch is the newest construction. I see from your notes that you'd like it restored, but I'm afraid it needs to be rebuilt. And don't worry, your bid already includes it."

"Fine, Rick. How soon can you get started?"

"Is this afternoon soon enough?" Rick asked, and again Paula noted his sparkling blue eyes. They seemed to dance with his enthusiasm, and she couldn't help but smile.

"Wonderful. The sooner you get started, the sooner I can

move in." Paula sighed happily. "I haven't been this excited about anything for five years."

"Five years?" Rick questioned. "Oh, excuse me, it's none of my business."

"Don't give it a second thought. You see, my husband passed away five years ago."

Rick nodded and gave her an empathetic smile. "My Olivia died eight years ago."

"Your wife?" Paula asked.

"Yes."

"Rick, does it get easier?" She tilted her head and gave him her full attention.

"Yes, I guess so. The memories are always there, but the pain eventually goes away. I know Olivia is in a better place, and what more could I want for her?"

Paula looked at Rick in a different light. At first, she considered him more of a country fellow simply showing off his best manners to impress her, but now she viewed him in a new perspective. Rick didn't hesitate to say he was a Christian. Actually he declared it with no hesitation. Paula admired a man who boldly talked about the Lord. It said a great deal about his character.

Barbara had been right about her assessment of Rick's looks. He stood trim and in great shape for his age and was definitely handsome.

I like his eyes the best, Paula decided. *He's warm, friendly, and very patient. I'm sure we will work together well. John would have been pleased. Rick has a good reputation for quality work, and I believe he'll live up to our agreement. Now, if only Kristi could accept my decision on this project.*

three

"So tell me how your meeting went," Barbara demanded. Paula heard the curiosity in her best friend's voice and traveled another mile while she squirmed for information.

"You mean the meeting with Mr. Davenport?" Paula asked innocently.

"The one and only," Barbara said. "I'm dying to hear all about it."

"It went just fine. I now have a better understanding of the electrical wiring and plumbing going into the house."

"That's all?" Barbara asked, disbelief lacing her words. "You were there in the house alone for over an hour!"

"In a business meeting," Paula reminded her. "Remember our earlier conversation about men?"

"Oh yes, I do, but just because you have resolved yourself to spend the rest of your life alone, doesn't mean God has the same plans."

Paula shook her head. "Not this time, Barb, and certainly not with Rick Davenport. I'm simply and absolutely not interested." She heard her friend mumble something. "What?"

"Oh, nothing," Barbara replied, reaching across the car and patting her lightly on the shoulder. "I was only getting in the last word."

The two laughed, and their conversation reverted to the renovation of the farmhouse—the magnitude of the project and the decorating plans. Paula felt even more pleased with her purchase. Today she could visualize completion of some of the rooms. Color schemes and themes rolled around in her head as she slowly developed more decorating ideas. All of the antiques she had collected over the years would now have a proper home.

"Comfortably country," she explained to Barbara, "with a

touch of Victorian but homey and inviting." Paula wanted her guests to feel relaxed, from the homemade chocolate chip cookies awaiting their arrival to the soft sounds of old hymns playing throughout the downstairs.

Paula picked up the cell phone on the car seat beside her. "I need to call Kristi; it's been nearly a week since I last talked to her. She hasn't returned my E-mail messages or the reminders I left on her answering machine."

"Maybe she's busy at work," Barbara suggested.

"You could be right," Paula said, placing the phone to her ear. "But our relationship leaves a lot to be desired lately, and I want to keep in touch."

"She still doesn't like the idea of the bed-and-breakfast?" Barbara asked, shaking her head.

"No, and I hope she's in a better mood." Suddenly an idea struck her, and she perked with the thought. "We're about twenty minutes from home; maybe the three of us could have dinner together."

"Sounds good to me," Barbara chimed in. "I haven't visited with Kristi in ages."

Paula punched the numbers into the phone and waited for her daughter to answer. "Hi, honey. How are you?"

Paula felt her stomach churn with Kristi's curt response and reluctantly laid the phone beside her.

"That was quick," Barbara said, breaking the silence between them.

Bursting into unexpected tears, she accepted a tissue from her friend and dabbed her eyes. "I'm sorry, I don't know what came over me."

"Well, I can guess," Barbara said dryly. "Miss Kristi must have been in one of her bad moods."

Paula blew her nose. "The worst I've seen, and she made it clear that she didn't want to talk to me. She really hurt my feelings, but now I'm getting angry."

Barbara handed her another tissue. "What happened?"

"Well, my precious daughter informed me that if I didn't have an appointment or if my call wasn't an emergency not to bother her at work." Paula pressed her lips together in an effort to keep from crying.

"Whew!" Barbara exclaimed, sitting straight up. "I'd like to march over to her little office and paddle her behind."

Paula smiled through her tears. "And when you're finished, I'll take a swing, too." She paused to consider her deep concern for Kristi. "You know I love her so much, Barb. Nothing she can do will destroy my feelings, but maybe it's time for me to break ties until she sees things differently. It will utterly devastate me, but I've felt God moving me in this direction for the past several months."

Barbara gave her friend a sympathetic look. "Oh Paula, I know how hard you've prayed for Kristi. And I can only imagine how difficult it would be for you to cease contact. I'll continue to pray for God to lead you in the right direction."

Paula took a deep breath. "Thank you. The situation has grown steadily worse since John died. Kristi refuses counseling, and she isolates herself from all of her old friends. This obsession of hers for money and power really frightens me. It all points to a grieving child of God who has forsaken her heavenly Father. She's said some pretty rough things to me lately about the bed-and-breakfast. My daughter has become bitter and unhappy."

"I agree," Barbara said. "Kristi just doesn't seem to be herself."

"Can we pray about this before I take you home?" Paula asked, feeling the tears fill her eyes again.

"How about right now?" Barbara asked gently, and when Paula agreed, she began. "Heavenly Father, we know You love Kristi more than we could ever imagine. We are at a loss as to what to do or say. She's all grown up, Lord, and John and Paula raised her in a Christian home. Somewhere along the way she's strayed from You. We need wisdom in what You want for Kristi's life. In Jesus' name, Amen."

"Thanks," Paula whispered, reaching for her friend's hand. "I don't know what I'd do without you."

"I think we're just stuck together." Barbara gave her a

reassuring smile. "By the way, when did Kristi last attend church?"

Paula sighed heavily; she knew the answer. "Not since John's funeral."

❧

Paula's heart felt heavy as the pastor concluded his message on reconciliation and asked for an altar call. She needed prayer and stepped forward to meet one of the ministers.

"Would you pray with me?" she asked softly. "My daughter isn't walking with the Lord, and I need guidance on how to handle family matters."

The minister took her hand and prayed for direction in Paula's relationship with Kristi. He asked for strength, wisdom, and trust in the Lord's perfect holy plan. In those final moments of prayer, Paula heard God speak to her heart. She wept and accepted His will for her life and Kristi's.

Upon leaving church, Barbara and Wade waited for Paula. They had both committed themselves to prayer for Kristi and wanted to know if they could do more.

"You are already doing what is best," Paula said, hoping she sounded braver than she felt. "Thank you for being my friends. You two have always been there for me, and I love you dearly. Just knowing you care makes me feel better."

"This should be a high point in your life, making all the plans for your bed-and-breakfast," Wade said, and folded his arms across his chest. He stood over six feet tall and his stance alone caused one to take notice. "Instead you are bombarded by criticism rather than support."

Paula smiled sadly. "Oddly enough, the more objections I hear, the more determined I am to make The Country Charm succeed. God planted the seed of this bed-and-breakfast long before John died, and I intend to follow through with it."

"Bravo," Wade said. "Barbara and I will be your first guests."

❧

When Paula returned home from church, a message awaited her on the answering machine. Hoping it was Kristi, she pressed the play button.

"Hi, Paula, this is Rick Davenport," the deep voice announced, and she turned up the volume. "I apologize for bothering you on a Sunday, but I do have a question. It looks as though I will be in Austin in the morning, and I wondered if you would be interested in looking at kitchen cabinets. You can page me at the number on my card. I'll be at home after church tonight, around seven-thirty, to return your page. Thanks."

Paula saved the message. She enjoyed hearing Rick's voice, warm and friendly just like his personality. Her mind wandered back to his rich, throaty laugh and the way his smile seemed almost contagious. *I wonder if he has a special girlfriend,* she mused. *Not that I'm interested.*

Paula spent the afternoon thoroughly engrossed in planning her new bedroom and bath, kitchen, utility room, pantry, and a half-bath from pictures gathered over the years. Her array of decorating ideas had migrated from the dining room table to the living room floor, where she had more space. She knew exactly what would fit within the dimensions of her bedroom since she planned to use her own assortment of antique cherry bedroom furniture complete with a high, four-poster bed. Paula pictured a white crocheted canopy draped over the four posts with an arrowhead pattern quilt in blue, yellow, and touches of green. She had a collection of quilts that her mother had passed down to her. They were all stitched by hand, and she wanted to use them all. To complete the room, she'd add throw pillows, dried flowers, pieces of antique baby clothes, and two more quilts.

"And I love my new kitchen," she said aloud and clapped her hands, feeling like a delighted child.

The red, green, and yellow sunflower decor was exactly how she envisioned a country kitchen. She also decided on the same color scheme for the half-bath, pantry, and utility room.

Paula stood and paced across the living room. Rick had told her the back sunporch must be totally rebuilt. She easily envisioned guests having morning coffee or breakfast seated in a sunny area overlooking a garden of green plants and flowers. Suddenly she recalled a picture she had recently clipped from a country decorating magazine. Flipping through the mound of files containing over ten years of findings, Paula found her sunporch. Hardwood floors, red paneled walls, furniture pieces painted in green and white, a sofa and chair covered in white denim, and blue granite accent pieces. Perfect. Absolutely perfect.

"Oh God, You are so good!" Paula exclaimed, then she laughed. John had always told her that one day she'd get caught talking to herself.

four

Paula saw Rick's truck pull into her driveway, and she grabbed her purse and keys. A strange tingling sensation swept through her at the sight of him, and she hesitated to open the door. *Where did this feeling come from?* she asked herself. *I've been listening too much to Barbara's matchmaking ideas.*

"Hi, Rick," Paula greeted and opened wide the door. Instantly the fresh scent of spring met her. "Isn't this a beautiful morning?"

"Yes, ma'am, it is," Rick said, and Paula thought his drawl suited him just fine. "I smell spring, and I'm ready for it. Don't know about you, but I'm tired of gray days and the cold biting at my heels."

Paula smiled and caught a glimpse of Rick's blue eyes. "Me, too. I like color and growing things around me. I can only imagine what it will be like at my farmhouse." Suddenly Paula felt an intense desire for her life to leap ahead.

"Um," Rick said with a smile. "You will love the bluebonnets. They'll be in full bloom by next month." He opened the truck door for her, and she stepped inside.

Suddenly Paula remembered her manners. "Rick, thanks for offering to take me to your vendors today. I really appreciate it."

His eyes danced, and she caught her reflection in them. "My pleasure," he replied before shutting the door.

Once inside, Rick checked a key map before they pulled away from the curb. "I searched the web last night for your red cabinets and found a closeout sale on what you described."

"Wonderful," Paula said, feeling a little warm sitting next to Rick. "I thought I'd have to buy unfinished cabinets and paint them myself."

"Not if I can help it," Rick grinned. "And I found out some

more good news. This vendor also carries countertops and usually at a good price." He picked up some papers on the seat
between them. "I printed out prices and sizes for the cabinets
and a separate sheet for countertops."

"Do you always go to this much trouble for your clients?"
Paula asked, scanning the computer printout.

Rick chuckled. "Well, I try to do my best. Of course, your
place has a soft spot in my heart, and it will be fun watching
you fix it up."

Paula laughed softly. "Sometimes it's a bit overwhelming."

The truck slowed to a halt at a stoplight. He glanced her way
and flashed a big smile. "I think you could do just about anything you set your mind to. You remind me of my grandmother. If she felt God wanted her to do something, then
nothing stood in her way."

"Sounds like she and I fall under the category of stubborn."

"Maybe so, but oh my, was she a gentle lady. Speaking of
my grandmother, I've got a little something for you." He
reached inside his shirt pocket and produced a cross made from
two square nails tied with a piece of leather. "We pulled these
nails from your house and couldn't use them. I thought you
might like it."

Paula took the cross and turned it over in the palm of her
hand. "Rick, how can I thank you for such thoughtfulness? I
am touched by your gift. It really symbolizes my Christian
bed-and-breakfast. Thank you so much."

"I thought you might like it," he said simply. "I have a feeling God will bless your efforts—over and above what you've
ever dreamed."

Their conversation moved to his four children and three
grandchildren. He had pictures, and possibly over lunch he'd
show her, that is, if she would have lunch with him.

Paula didn't need to think twice. "I'd love to," she agreed.

She learned Rick took his granddaughters to Sunday
school and church each week. The girls' parents had fallen
away from the Lord, and he intended for his granddaughters
to know Jesus. He also volunteered in a class of three-year-

olds on Sunday morning.

"Those little ones keep me humble," Rick said. "They know and love Jesus simply, just like we all are supposed to do."

Paula nodded and decided she found a new admiration of Rick Davenport. She felt comfortable with her new friend, and she surprised herself by relaxing and enjoying his company.

Rick's vendor did have the perfect cabinets in stock and at an excellent price. The vendor claimed he didn't have much market for red kitchen cabinets, and if she purchased her countertops from him, he'd discount them even more.

She felt elated, and soon the kitchen specs were laid out for Paula, Rick, and the vendor to study. Rick helped her put the orders together, and he made it easy for her to select options and unique pieces. He pointed out what other folks had selected in homes he'd built and their comments on special designs.

"Take a look at these wall cabinets with glass doors," Rick pointed out. "If you lined a wall with them, you could display your dishes and glassware."

"Excellent idea," Paula agreed. She appreciated his suggestions. He didn't push his ideas or try to hurry her through the decision process. "And this corner cabinet has a revolving shelf for easy access," she added.

Once they completed the purchases, Rick asked her what kind of food she wanted for lunch. Together they decided on Italian. The restaurant proved busy with the lunch hour business group, so Paula and Rick found time to talk and see Rick's photographs of his grandchildren.

"This little girl has her grandpa's eyes," Paula pointed out while examining a photo.

Rick peered over her shoulder. "Does she?" he grinned. "I hadn't noticed."

Paula laughed at his teasing. "I bet. She probably has her grandpa wrapped around her little finger."

"I think they all do," he admitted. "Of course, I spoil them rotten. Do you want to see pictures of the two I take to Sunday school? I just happen to have their pictures tucked in my wallet."

Paula laughed again. She couldn't remember having so much fun in a long time. "Yes, I want to see all of your grandchildren."

Rick raised an eyebrow and chuckled. "Now, you've done it. I guess I'll have to spread out all of these pictures for you to see." He lifted an accordion of photos from his wallet, and Paula laughed until she thought her sides would split.

As soon as they finished viewing Rick's grandchildren, a hostess escorted them to a table. Paula thought their lunch flew by.

"Do you have time to look at flooring?" Rick asked as they finished coffee. Both had opted for decaf coffee instead of dessert.

"Oh yes," Paula said enthusiastically, "but I don't want to interrupt any of your plans."

"Believe me, you're not." His eyes danced. "This is my life, and what man in his right mind wouldn't want the company of a gracious, lovely woman?"

Paula felt herself blush and fought for words. It had been a long time since a man complimented her. "Thank you," she stammered. "I have nothing planned, and this is fun."

The afternoon passed quickly, and Rick dropped her off at home shortly before five. They had picked up samples of flooring, paint colors, and more wallpaper books. Paula regretted seeing the afternoon end.

"This has been a wonderful day," she said as Rick helped her carry samples to the door.

"I agree. I hope there will be many more of these." And his remark caused her stomach to take a flip.

"Thank you for lunch and everything you did today." Paula felt like a teenager again, telling her date good-bye at the door.

"No problem. When do you think you'll be at the farmhouse?" Rick asked while she fumbled with her keys.

"Possibly Thursday morning." She gave the door a nudge to open. Once inside, they set their samples on the living room floor. "Will I be in the way?" she asked.

"No, ma'am," he assured her. "I'll have at least one crew of men working and maybe two. I'll be in and out as I check on a number of projects I have going."

"Good. Hopefully I'll have some decisions made by then."

Rick looked around him and gave her an admiring glance. "Your home is beautiful; it looks like you."

"And what do I look like?" she asked shyly.

He studied the living room portion where they had set the samples. "See this picture?" he asked, pointing to a landscape over the fireplace. "The colors and the setting are you, comfortable, rather country…and very attractive."

"Why thank you," Paula said. "The artist is Larry Dyke. In my opinion he's the best in this part of the country."

"He's from Texas, isn't he?"

"Yes, are you familiar with his work?" she asked curiously.

"One of my sons has a couple of his golf pictures. I didn't realize he did other things."

"Oh yes, lovely landscapes," she laughed. "I have six of his prints, and they will all go into the bed-and-breakfast."

"You've decided to stick to calling it The Country Charm?"

"I kind of fell into the name, and the more I hear it, the more I like it."

Rick nodded. "I like it, too. And by the way, I do like your ideas for decorating, not that my opinion means anything."

"Yes, it does!" she interrupted. "I'm sure you have seen a lot of good and bad decorating in your business. So, thanks for the compliment."

Rick stuck his hands in his jeans pockets. "Well, guess I'd better get back to Brenham. Thank you for running around with me today."

"Thank you for taking me," Paula replied, then paused thoughtfully. "Would you like to stay for dinner?"

"Oh, it's tempting," he said slowly, "but I have an appointment later on tonight. I will take a rain check, though. What about having lunch with me on Thursday?"

Paula nodded. "I think that would be just fine."

"I'll see you then," he said as she opened the door for him. Never had she seen such sparkling blue eyes, and Paula felt her heart skip a beat.

I'm acting like a silly schoolgirl, she chided. *I hope he can't tell. Oh, I would be so embarrassed.*

❧

Paula flipped through the floor samples, mentally picturing each one with the furnishings she planned to use at the bed-and-breakfast. Finally, she settled on a shade of oak, which enhanced the style of the old farmhouse. Marked pages of wallpaper books and corresponding paint samples rested next to the flooring. Just when she thought she had reached a deci-sion on paper and paint, Rick's image and bits and pieces of conversation floated across her mind.

What is the matter with me? she scolded. *Am I so lonely that I have mistaken his kindness for interest?* True, Paula hadn't considered another man since John's death, not that a few hadn't pursued her, but no one had sparked her attention until she met Rick.

"And he is nothing more than a friend," she said, then cringed when the cat meowed and scurried out of the room. "Sorry, Tapestry," she called after the pet. "Didn't mean to scare you." The gray, white, and tan cat cautiously walked back into the living room and snuggled up under Paula's arm. She fondly scratched behind Tapestry's ears.

"We do just fine by ourselves," Paula said softly. "But he is very nice. You would like him; he's kind and gentle." The memory of silver hair against a tan face caused her to smile. "Enough of this," Paula announced to the cat. "I have work to do."

Snatching the pencil from behind her ear, she went to work scribbling down paint numbers and names of wallpaper pat-terns. Two hours later, with quilts and wall hangings spread across the floor, the phone rang.

"It's me, Barbara. I just had to find out about your day."

"You mean visiting showrooms?" Paula asked, suppressing a laugh.

"Well, yes. Did you find kitchen cabinets?"

"Sure did, and countertops, too, and all at a great price,"

Paula said excitedly, seating herself in the middle of her decorating musings.

"And did Rick take you to all of those places?"

"Yes, ma'am."

"And?" Barbara prodded.

Paula laughed. "You are a case. I had a wonderful day picking out things for the house, and Rick did a great job chauffeuring me around to his vendors."

"Oh, I'm so happy for you," Barbara murmured.

"Me, too," Paula said happily. "I never dreamed I'd find exactly what I wanted. . .at such a great price," she hastily added.

"And I'm so pleased that you spent the entire day with Rick," Barbara said with a giggle. "So, are you interested?"

"Barbara, I am not in the market for a husband or boyfriend. Remember our earlier discussions about him?" Paula tried hard to sound believable.

"Yes, I recall every word, but I'm not sure John wanted you to live the rest of your life alone."

"What about God? He may feel I am right where He wants me to be," Paula pointed out.

"My point," Barbara said. "Think about it, dear friend. God has a reason for everything that happens to us. The man is single, Christian, attentive, kind, and gentle. What more could you ask?"

"A word from God? Even if I were to become serious with someone, Kristi would have a fit," Paula said.

"She has a fit on a daily basis," Barbara replied. "Oh, I'm sorry; I shouldn't have been so blunt."

"Heavens, don't think twice about it. You're right; she has blinders on when it comes to her mother."

"Has she called?"

"No. Let's not talk about Kristi or Rick," Paula said. "Let me tell you all about the things I have strewn across my living room floor. I'm having the time of my life with the samples over here. I wish you could see the mess in my living room."

"I could spare an hour. Wade has a church meeting tonight.

Can I come over? I won't bring up a single romantic notion."

"I don't believe that for a minute, but come on over. I need the help." Paula replaced the phone and folded her arms across her chest. She contemplated the day with Rick and felt some apprehension. The idea of a relationship frightened her. She sighed deeply. *Oh, John, I loved you so much. When you died you took part of my heart with you, and I don't ever want to face that kind of hurt again.*

five

Paula watched the sunrise on Thursday morning as she drove to Brenham. Already dawn promised a warm day without a single cloud in the sky. Arriving before the workers, Paula seized the opportunity to walk around the outside of the farmhouse and dream. She decided the rotted back porch did look bad and replacing it made a lot of sense. Once the house was finished, she'd need a professional landscaper. A green thumb had never been one of her attributes. She could manage a few indoor houseplants that required little care, but nothing outside.

Lifting hazel eyes, she focused her attention upon the rickety barn. Rick said it should be torn down before someone got hurt, and she agreed. He'd given her plans for a new structure, which contained horse stables, an area for a carriage and a wagon, and implement storage. Possibly, later she'd add some animals for a petting zoo.

"Halloo," she heard and turned to wave at Rick walking toward her.

"Good morning," Paula greeted. "I didn't hear you pull up; my thoughts were on the new barn."

Rick laughed and shook his head. "I don't know many people who get excited about a barn."

"To tell you the truth, I was thinking about the animals."

"Well, animals are why I've gotten a late start today."

Paula lifted a questioning brow.

"My son's collie gave birth to five puppies last night, and my grandson insisted I see them first thing this morning."

"Oh, collie puppies," Paula breathed. "Would they want to sell one of them?"

"For sure. When you have time, we can go see them." His eyes lingered on her face for a brief moment before he hastily turned to the back of the house. "While we're out here, where do you want the gazebo?"

Paula tapped her chin thoughtfully. "It depends. Can you suggest a good spot for a vegetable garden?"

Rick walked toward an area adjacent to the barn. "My grandmother had hers here. The soil is rich and fertile, so it should give you a good garden."

"Okay. Well, it's a project for next spring, and I'll have to take lessons so I won't kill the vegetables. Now what about the gazebo? I was thinking of directly in front of the sunporch."

"Sounds perfect to me. And you want it wired for electricity and mounted speakers?"

"Right. Can you tell I get more excited as the days pass?" Paula asked as a hint of a breeze picked up an auburn strand of hair and twisted it around her ear.

"I sure can. Do you like surprises?" Rick asked unexpectedly.

"Love them." She started to say John had been the master of surprises, but thought better of it.

Rick ran his fingers through his hair. "I'm a little embarrassed, and I hope I don't offend you, but I picked up a little something for you yesterday. I mean, if you don't care for it, that's fine."

"Well. . .what is it?" Paula asked, her eyes wide.

He pointed with his head. "Follow me over to the back of· my truck. It's sitting in there."

Paula felt like running, except she didn't want to appear too exuberant, so she forced herself to slow down to a fast walk.

"Here it is," Rick announced, pointing to an antique in the truck.

Paula gasped. "A spinning wheel! Oh my! Oh my!" She stepped onto the running board of the pickup for a better view. "It's beautiful; it's absolutely beautiful. I've always dreamed of a spinning wheel, but. . .Oh, Rick, what a beautiful surprise!"

"So you like it?" he asked, laughing at her glee.

"Absolutely, and this is the real thing," she went on. Paula reached out and touched it as though it couldn't be real. "So big, too. Can't you imagine a pioneer woman sitting here spinning thread?"

"Sure can," Rick said, surprising her with his comment.

"You can?"

"Yes, because it belonged to my great-grandmother."

Paula's hand flew to her mouth. "Oh, you don't dare part with it. It should go to one of your children."

"Nonsense. None of them care a whit about antiques. That's why I'm giving it to you. I'm pleased you like it."

Paula wanted to reach out and hug him for the gift, but she didn't dare. "I don't know what to say, except thank you," she breathed.

"Thanks is fine. . .and say you'll have lunch with me."

"Only if you let me buy," Paula said matter-of-factly.

"No, ma'am. I don't go for modern notions of women paying for men's meals. But I haven't forgotten your invitation for dinner, and I'll cash in your rain check after you get settled."

Paula felt a slow blush rise from her neck to her cheeks as Rick reached up to help her down from the running board.

"It makes me feel good to meet a woman who is both appreciative and beautiful," he drawled softly.

Paula knew her blush had turned to crimson.

&

"I've probably bothered you with this before, but when will I be able to move in?" Paula asked over a homemade chicken salad sandwich and a bowl of creamy potato soup.

"You need to have the kitchen area, your bedroom, and bath completed, right?" Rick asked as he set his glass of iced tea on the table.

Paula nodded. "Am I whining? Because if I am, I apologize."

"You're just anxious, and I don't blame you a bit. Now, to answer your question. I'd say, let's wait six weeks; maybe sooner, but we've ordered things that need to arrive before we can install them."

"I'll do better at being patient." Paula then remembered his gift. "Rick, the spinning wheel is wonderful. I thank you so very much."

Rick picked up the napkin in his lap and wiped his mouth. She could see he concealed a smile. He leaned over the table and whispered. "I sure like the look on your face when you're happy. The light in your eyes would put the sun to shame."

Paula didn't know quite how to reply. "Do you always pour lavish compliments on all of your lady clients?" she asked lightly, reaching for her iced tea.

Rick shook his head and hesitated before speaking. "No, I don't. . .Truthfully, it has been a while since I spent time with a single lady. Does it bother you?"

"Not exactly, I just wondered why."

He took a deep breath. "I'll be more careful of what I say, especially if it offends you."

"No, Rick, of course not. I want you to be yourself," Paula insisted. She couldn't figure out why her heart raced, and she knew the telltale blush had arrived again. Why did she allow him to do this to her?

"Paula," he began slowly.

She lifted hazel eyes to meet warm, liquid blues.

"I really would like to drive into Austin tomorrow evening and take a certain lady to dinner and a movie. Do you suppose she'd accept?"

"She might." Paula returned the smile.

"She's a beautiful, redhead lady with the prettiest eyes," he continued. "But I'm afraid she'd say no."

Paula tilted her head slightly, wanting the bantering to go on, but not sure what to say next. She hesitated. "I think she'd say yes."

"Do you suppose I could pick her up around seven o'clock?"

"Seven is fine. Where are you taking the lady so she knows what to wear?"

This time Rick paused. "It's a secret, but someplace nice. You know, like you'd wear to church."

"I see," she said laughing. "I. . .I mean the lady will be ready."

The rest of their lunch centered on conversation about the farmhouse. Paula eased a sigh of relief and contemplated telling Rick he shouldn't be interested in her. Each time she found the courage to bring up the topic, something stopped her.

All afternoon Paula considered their lunch. As she wandered from room to room and made notes on style and furnishings, she pondered over a relationship with Rick. Lately, he took front stage of most of her thoughts, and it frustrated her. She admitted to liking his charming ways, even if his words sounded a bit corny.

You have a business to put together, she scolded herself. *Get your priorities straight.*

Before long, her mind turned to Rick again. She walked into the library, where the spinning wheel now sat. How sweet of him to give it to her. And this had been his great-grandmother's! Paula wondered if he habitually gave extravagant gifts. She'd like to think not. In fact, she hoped his generous gift had been thought out and not impulsive.

Paula kneeled to carefully run her fingers over the spinning wheel. She couldn't find a flaw anywhere, and she wanted to place it in an ideal spot. Every room seemed to beckon, "Put the spinning wheel here."

Paula walked through the downstairs and saw a perfect alcove in the dining room. Already she envisioned an antique wall hanging of various threads and a basket on the floor. A cane chair would be perfect to accent the corner. She hoped Rick liked where she planned to place his gift.

At five o'clock the working crew announced their departure. Paula gathered up her samples and left with them. Rick didn't like the idea of her staying alone at the farmhouse in the evening until he installed a burglar alarm.

"Vandals might see the supplies in the back of the house, and I don't want you here while they help themselves," he said with a concerned frown. He lingered around the property until she packed up her sport utility vehicle and headed back to Austin.

As soon as she pulled into her own driveway, Kristi's European status symbol drove in behind her.

"Hi honey," Paula called, stepping from her car. "You're just in time to help me carry in samples for the bed-and-breakfast. I'm so ecstatic, and I can't wait to show you the plans."

Kristi stood frozen on the driveway. "You mean you already bought the place?" She arched her back and raised her chin stubbornly, just like she used to do when she was a little girl.

Paula feigned a smile. "Yes, and work is in progress."

"How could you purchase that piece of junk when you knew I didn't approve?" Kristi demanded.

Paula fought the temper wanting to take control of her words. *Lord, help me with this,* she prayed. *Fill me with Your words.* She wet her lips and captured Kristi's gaze.

"Kristi, I didn't need your approval to make this purchase," she said gently. "It is my business as to what I do with my money. I am perfectly capable of making sound business decisions."

"Even when it destroys my future?" Kristi fairly shouted.

"Unless you want the neighbors to hear you, you need to lower your voice." Turning her back, Paula proceeded to open her tailgate and lift out wallpaper books. Keys in hand, she walked toward the back door.

The young woman followed her. "Didn't you hear what I said? Or don't you care?"

"Care about your future?" Paula asked softly, fumbling with her keys. "Of course I do, but I don't see how my bed-and-breakfast affects your future. Maybe you need to explain it to me." Paula nodded to a kitchen chair. "Sit down, and calm down. I will listen to what you have to say as long as you talk respectfully."

"Oh, Mother, I'm an adult," Kristi said with a huff.

"And I am your mother."

Kristi rolled her eyes, but Paula ignored the gesture.

The young woman raised her chin. "The money you have invested could have been invested in my future."

"How?"

"By putting it aside so I could acquire my own brokerage firm," Kristi said simply. "Daddy would have wanted it for me."

Paula couldn't believe her ears. "Your father left you a large sum of money, Kristi—plenty to invest in whatever you desire."

"That's my money!" Kristi shouted. "The least you could do is plan for my future like Daddy did."

"Are you saying I owe you money?" Paula asked incredulously.

"In short, yes."

Paula sat down across from her and methodically folded her hands on the table. "I have no idea where you have gotten such an outlandish idea," she began. "But your father and I did not raise you to be selfish and demanding. Our Lord instructs us—"

"Mother, please. I have no desire to hear about your God. It doesn't mean a thing to me."

"When did this happen?" Paula asked with grave concern. "You were brought up in a Christian home. You were a part of family worship, and you made a decision for Christ."

"So. . .a lot of good religion did for Daddy. Sorry, but I have no use for God. It's a crutch for uneducated minds."

"Excuse me?" Paula heard her own voice raise.

"You heard me."

Again Paula wet her lips and considered her response. "I forgive you for what you just said to me, but I will not sit by while you insult our Lord. I love you and so does He. Perhaps you need to reflect upon your demands of me and your attitude toward the God of the universe."

Kristi stood and glared at her mother angrily. "I'm through talking to you, Mother, but this is not the end of the matter. You're naive and uninformed about what goes on in the real world, and I intend to have it stopped!"

Paula watched as Kristi left the room, slamming the door behind her. Normally she would have raced out after Kristi in a state of tears, but not tonight. Somewhere, somehow, her daughter had moved so far from the Lord that Paula could no longer reach her. She wasn't even sure what Kristi intended to have stopped—the real world or Paula's so-called naivete.

Oh Lord, John and I gave Kristi to You on the day she was born. She is Yours, Father; draw her back to Your fold. The trusting little girl who gave her heart to You has become bitter and cold. Only Your love can win her back. Amen.

This time Paula couldn't stop the lump in her throat. She sat at the kitchen table and willed the tears to stop, but they refused. Burying her face in her hands, Paula wept.

Shortly before nine, Paula dialed Barbara's number. It had been a long time since she'd called her friend with the grief she felt at this moment. All of the old feelings from when John died came rolling back.

"Hey, what's wrong?" Barbara asked. Just the sound of her friend's voice soothed her.

Paula explained the whole scene with Kristi, stopping twice to dab her eyes and blow her nose.

"She's worse than what we expected," Barbara said gently. "Can Wade and I pray with you right now?"

Paula listened for Wade to pick up the extension phone. For the next several minutes Wade and Barbara prayed for Kristi as well as wisdom for Paula. The sadness faded to hope as her friends assured her of God's love and protection over His own.

"Thank you," Paula said, her voice laced with emotion. "You two are like a lighthouse in a storm."

"We feel the same about you," Wade replied. "I'm going to let you ladies talk now. And remember, you call us day or night."

"Thanks, Wade," and Paula heard him hang up. "You have a gem," she informed Barbara.

"I agree. Say, how was the rest of your day?"

"Very good, actually. Work crews were there at the house, and I busied myself by planning and daydreaming."

"Did Rick stop by?"

The comment forced a smile from Paula. "Yes, he did. In fact, he brought me a gift and took me to lunch."

"Wonderful, Paula. What did he bring you?"

Paula could hear the enthusiasm in her voice. "Well, a spinning wheel."

"Oh my!" Barbara cried. "Did he have any idea how long you have wanted one?"

"No, but he did know the gift pleased me."

"So, *now* what are your feelings toward him?" Barbara asked softly.

Paula paused to contemplate her answer. "Hmm, I guess cautious, frightened, jittery, and very much like a teenage girl."

"I think you're being attacked by a virus called love."

Paula protested. "I keep telling myself I'm too old for such feelings."

"Is that what's stopping you?" her friend asked sincerely.

Barbara's question forced Paula to face the truth. "No, not really. I guess fear has a hold of my heart. I loved John and he died; I couldn't bear to lose someone again."

"Give it to God," Barbara suggested softly. "And I'll be praying for you."

six

Paula read her Bible and prayed until after midnight. She experienced the same peace given to her the Sunday morning she asked for prayer. God led her through the passages of hope and promise, and Psalm 139 comforted her like a soft quilt on a chilly night.

"Where can I go from your Spirit? Where can I flee from your presence? If I go up to the heavens, you are there; if I make my bed in the depths, you are there. If I rise on the wings of the dawn, if I settle on the far side of the sea, even there your hand will guide me, your right hand will hold me fast."

You can't run from God, Kristi, Paula thought, closing her Bible. *He knows where you are and what you're thinking. He will bring you back to Him.*

She picked up her prayer journal and read through the many times that she had asked God to hear her deepest prayers. Beside the entry was listed the date God answered her. He would again, too; she only needed to wait. The last two verses of the psalm, ones she had memorized as a child, spoke to her again just as she drifted off to sleep.

"Search me, O God, and know my heart; test me and know my anxious thoughts. See if there is any offensive way in me, and lead me in the way everlasting."

❧

Paula studied her appearance from the top of her head to her black patent leather pumps. She felt like a sixteen-year-old waiting on her first date. Makeup looked okay; not overdone, but she wouldn't be washed out in dim lights, either. Thick, auburn hair, layered and stylishly cut, touched her shoulders. She'd selected a forest green silk suit with a lightweight black knit sweater. Fumbling through her jewelry box, she added her pearl earrings, bracelet, and necklace.

Glancing at the clock, she realized Rick would be arriving in less than fifteen minutes. A case of nerves unleashed and Paula wondered if she'd chosen the proper outfit. Suddenly it occurred to her that her favorite cologne might be too strong. What if he had an allergic reaction to the scent?

She caught herself frowning in the mirror and replaced it with a smile. Worrying herself over her clothes, cologne, and makeup solved nothing. Besides, God didn't want His children feeling anxious about anything. She'd know in an instant whether Rick approved, and deep down she hoped he'd be pleased.

For a moment she regretted accepting the dinner invitation. Maybe she should be considering the circumstances with Kristi instead of rushing off to have a good time. It looked as though she didn't care about her daughter, but nothing could be further from the truth. Her heart felt heavy, wishing with all her might that the two could resolve their differences.

Breathing a prayer, Paula walked away from the mirror to wait until Rick arrived. She felt disoriented and unsure of herself. After all, she'd married John at age twenty, and times had changed—except she and Rick shared the same religious convictions. The bond of Christianity alone calmed her frazzled nerves.

I wonder if Rick is as nervous as I am.

&

Rick changed his tie for the third time. Two suits and another sports jacket lay across his bed. He needed to snatch up his keys and head for Austin, but none of his ties looked right with his brown tweed sports coat. Tearing off the jacket, he quickly changed into a western cut tan suit, white shirt, and a navy, tan, and brown tie.

Rick hadn't had a date since he married Olivia at age twenty-three, and he questioned the wisdom of doing it all again. He dumped out a seldom-used wooden box where he stored cuff links and a few pieces of jewelry. Slipping on a rather large gold nugget ring and a Swiss watch, Rick took a good look at himself in the mirror.

I don't think so, he muttered, tearing off the watch and ring. Instead he picked up a familiar dress watch and felt much more comfortable. Checking the time, he headed for the door, wondering why in the world he had asked Paula Franklin out to dinner and a movie.

"Move over, Spurs," Rick said to his golden retriever. "I'm drivin' into the big city for a date with a pretty lady."

I feel like a wet-nosed kid, he thought. *Lord, are You sure this is part of Your plan? I mean, she's a wonderful lady and I like her a lot, but I feel like a fool.*

With his truck moving in the direction of Austin, Rick checked the clock on his dash. He had enough time to pick up Paula and make it to a favorite restaurant, Ruth's Steak House, for their seven-thirty reservations. A smile spread across his face. If he drove a little faster, he could bring the lady flowers. He bet she'd like roses, a whole dozen red ones.

Calm down, old man, he told himself. *This is the same lady who made such a fuss over your great-grandmother's spinning wheel. She's different, extra-special different.*

Rick pounded the steering wheel with the palm of his hand. He'd forgotten his medicine. Lifting up the console, he found another bottle for those times when he neglected to take the prescription.

࠲

"This is my favorite restaurant," Paula said, smiling across the table at Rick.

"Good, mine, too. I'd hoped this would be to your liking," Rick said, noticeably nervous.

"And the roses are lovely," Paula added. "I'm certainly not used to all of this pampering."

"Your other men friends should be ashamed of themselves," Rick chuckled.

Paula wondered if she ought to tell him the truth. She hesitated. "I think you should know that I have not dated since my late husband."

Rick picked up his glass of iced tea and hesitated. "Truthfully, I haven't gone out since my wife died, either."

They both laughed.

"I'm not sure how I'm supposed to act, so you let me know if I embarrass you," Rick said. "My dating days consisted of a drive-in movie, popcorn, and a cherry cola."

"Did you wear your hair slicked back and a black leather jacket?" Paula asked with a gentle laugh.

"No, ma'am, I've always been a cowboy. No rock and roll for me; I lived and breathed country music, mostly gospel. What about you?"

"Oh, bobby socks, a poodle skirt, and a ponytail," she sighed. "I loved Elvis Presley."

"And you call yourself a Texas girl?" Rick teased.

"Of course, a well-rounded Texas girl," she pointed out.

"By the way," he began, once they finished laughing. "Thank you for accepting my invitation tonight."

"Well, I'm flattered and very appreciative of your attention," Paula said shyly. "Thank you for everything you've done for me, Rick. I mean, you have made my dream of a Christian bed-and-breakfast near reality."

Rick reached across the table and grasped her hand. "I'm glad you're pleased. It's a comforting thought to know my grandma's home will bless the lives of others. She loved having people visit, and I still remember the way she always praised God for good friends."

"More of us could take lessons from old-fashioned hospitality," Paula said softly, enjoying the feel of his hand over hers. "I hope to bring some of that to The Country Charm. My desire is to have all of my guests feel the presence of God and His love."

"And they will," Rick replied. "I'm sure of it."

Paula chatted constantly during the rest of their meal. She noticed he seemed nervous, but as they talked, he eased into the Rick Davenport she knew.

Fortunately the movie was rated PG, and Paula didn't have to make a stand against its rating. As she thought about it, she couldn't imagine Rick escorting her to any inappropriate movie. The lighthearted comedy on the screen topped the evening, and they both laughed till tears rolled down their faces.

Once the movie ended, the two left the theater hand in hand. Paula hadn't been this happy and content in a long time. Over coffee, they talked about their children and how they tried to reverse the role of a parent-child relationship.

Rick chuckled. "One of my daughters calls me every other day to make sure I'm eating right, exercising, and getting enough sleep."

"Sounds like the calls we made to them when they were in college," Paula said.

Rick nodded. "I'm glad they care and haven't absorbed themselves completely in their own lives. I see too much self-centeredness in young people."

Paula thought about her relationship to Kristi. Caring had nothing to do with her daughter's attitude.

"Rick, were all of your children raised in a Christian home?" Paula asked, hoping her question didn't give away her concerns over Kristi.

"Yes, and all four have stayed with the Lord, except one. Andy married an unbeliever thinking he could influence her to make a decision for the Lord." His eyes darkened. "But, he hasn't been successful. In fact, he rarely attends church. Now, those granddaughters of mine are convicting them both by talking about Jesus."

Paula took a sip of her coffee. "You have a good life, don't you, Rick?" she asked softly, raising her eyes to meet his.

"It's good, but not full. What about you? I hope I'm not out of line, but whenever you mention your daughter, I see a lot of sadness in your face."

Paula fought hard to conceal the pain. "She's turned her back on the Lord and me. She's become very selfish, and it hurts."

Rick reached across the small table and grasped her hand again, the second time of the evening. His gentle touch nearly brought her to tears.

"I really believe when those we love turn their backs on the Lord and also reject us, it's because they see the Lord in us. It frustrates them. When we show them unconditional love and follow God's ways, they want us to quarrel and fall away from everything right and true."

"I never heard it said quite that way before," Paula sighed, grateful for the compassionate nature of Rick Davenport.

"And the Lord will be victorious over them; we only need to keep praying and believing in His word."

"Patience is a difficult virtue," Paula said with a sad smile. "Thank you for putting my feelings into words. I truly feel better."

Rick squeezed her hand lightly before releasing it. "And I'm always happy to lend a hand or a prayer."

seven

"Don't you dare open your eyes," Rick warned. He opened the passenger side of his truck and reached for Paula's hand. "Do I need to blindfold you?" he asked sternly. "Because I have a bandana in my pocket."

Four weeks had passed since their dinner and movie in Austin, and the two had become close friends.

"Maybe you'd better," Paula said laughing. "I might peek."

She heard Rick give a labored sigh. "All right, stand up while I tie this on. It's a good thing I have a clean bandana."

Paula wrinkled her nose. "I guess I should consider myself lucky."

She stood while Rick reached behind her to tie the cloth. The woodsy smell of his aftershave touched her senses.

"You smell wonderful," he whispered. "Enough to drive a man crazy."

"I was thinking the same thing about you," Paula murmured.

"You're blushing," he accused. "And I like it." He whirled her around. "Now I am going to lead you into the house."

"I'm dying to see what you've done," Paula said. "Let's hurry."

Rick did not intend to rush her. Slowly they walked around the truck and on toward the house. She heard the workers laughing, and someone hammered away.

"Here's the first step," Rick instructed, "and here's three more."

The screen door screeched and shut behind them. Paula recognized the jolly voice of the Hispanic foreman who greeted both of them.

"Good morning, Lupe," she said.

"And good morning to you," Lupe replied, then laughed. "You look like you could use some help."

"Now Rick?" Paula questioned. "Can I see what you've done?"

"Um, not yet. Everything has to be just right; maybe today is not good. I could easily take you back to Austin," Rick teased.

"But you won't because I promised you a home-cooked meal tonight."

"What a hard bargain you drive," Rick said with a sigh. "Okay, you win." He reached to untie the bandana.

Paula opened her eyes and clapped her hands with joy at the sight of the kitchen. Not only were the hardwood floors installed, but also the cabinets and the countertops. In her enthusiasm, she whirled completely around taking in the sight of the room.

"Oh my, oh my. It's absolutely lovely," Paula breathed. "And the woodwork is stripped, too. Oh, look at the floor, and the cabinets are more beautiful than I ever anticipated. I'm so glad I chose green countertops. Oh, Rick, what a wonderful surprise!" She glanced at boxes stacked beside the cast iron stove. "And my wallpaper is here, too. Thank you ever so much." Paula whirled around to see Rick's smiling face. Their eyes met briefly, and she saw the familiar twinkle.

"I guess I don't have to ask if you're pleased," he said with a chuckle. "So I'll just say you're welcome, and pass it on to the crew."

Paula looked all around; several of the crew stood watching her response. She instantly blushed crimson at their amusement over her excitement. "Thanks, guys. You all have been so good putting up with me. How about if I bring lunch on Friday, maybe a barbecue brisket, potato salad, home-made rolls, fresh green beans, and a couple of strawberry pies?"

The echoes of approval rang throughout the house.

"We might never finish this project," Lupe said.

Still laughing, the men dispersed and Paula scrutinized every corner of the kitchen. To her delight, the half-bath and pantry were completed. She felt her eyes moisten. *Thank You, Lord. I'm not worthy for the many blessings You have*

given me. Thank You for loving me, and thank You for such a
good friend as Rick.

Opening her eyes, Paula once more glanced around the kitchen. On the other side of the room, Rick stood with his hands in his pockets leaning against the doorway.

"I was thanking the Lord," she said softly.

He nodded knowingly. "I could tell by the look on your face."

"He is so good, Rick. When I think about the problems we've encountered and all of the ones which will surely happen, I'm certain God has blessed our work," Paula hesitated, wanting her words to convey exactly how she felt. "None of this has been easy, and I don't think I would want it to be. God honors hard work, and I do want this bed-and-breakfast to be a blessing to everyone who works on it."

Rick sauntered over to Paula's side. She met an ineffable glance that sent her senses reeling. "I believe you are my blessing," he whispered.

Without deliberating the consequences of exposing her own emotions, she gazed directly into his eyes.

"Scary, isn't it?" Rick asked softly.

Paula trembled and instantly broke the moment between them by walking toward the box of wallpaper. "Yes, it is," she replied barely above a whisper.

"Can we talk about this tonight?" Rick's voice seemed to consume her.

She realized facing him would bring her inmost emotions to the surface again, so she bent to examine the wallpaper instead. "I suppose we should," she managed.

≈

While Rick tended to business, Paula admired every inch of her new cabinetry in the kitchen, bath, and pantry. She marveled at the size of the pantry and pictured cupboards and shelves lined with jars of homemade vegetables, fruits, jellies, and pickles. Everything at The Country Charm would be homemade, just like food used to be prepared, except the bread. Paula adored her bread machine; perhaps she'd concede to one modern technique. Well, maybe two; she wasn't ready to milk a cow for fresh milk, butter, and cottage cheese either.

Paula caught a glimpse of Rick and the foreman walking across the area where the old barn stood. She remembered Rick started each day with prayer and wondered how the men felt about it. From what she'd seen and heard, his men respected their boss. Rick lifted a pad of paper from underneath his arm and showed the foreman some notes. No doubt they were arranging to tear down the barn. She knew Rick planned to have the crew demolish it next week.

Her heart soared at the sight of him. No longer did she feel intimidated by schoolgirl feelings. The emotions were honest, and nothing to be ashamed or denied, only cautious. She loved his surprises, and he claimed to enjoy seeing her reactions.

When John died, Paula believed she could never love again. The hurt and the gnawing ache tore at her for two solid years. John's heart had failed him, but her own suffered irreparable damage. Now things were easier. She still missed him, but God had given her peace and comfort.

The thought of loving another man seemed more than scary; in fact, she felt terrified. Burying one husband had been enough, but what about this relationship with Rick? She and John had dated for two years before they were sure of their love and God's plan for their lives. Rick Davenport had been in her life for two months, and already she felt him tugging at her heartstrings. They hadn't spoken of the growing tenderness between them until today, and his comment brought hidden emotions to the surface.

Rick said he hadn't dated since his wife's death. Why, and why now? Only God knew those answers, and for the present, she must rest in the knowledge of His perfect plan.

Late that afternoon Rick drove Paula back to Austin. Neither of them mentioned the words exchanged earlier in the day. They skirted around every topic and issue but their relationship.

❧

"You grill a mean steak," Rick declared. "If tonight's meal is any indication of what you will be cooking for folks at the bed-and-breakfast, then you'll run your competitors out of business."

Paula beamed. "I'm glad you enjoyed it, and I did make dessert even though I noticed you never eat any."

"Um," Rick said thoughtfully. "What did you make?"

"Homemade angel food cake with fresh strawberries."

He grinned. "Perfect. It's not that I don't enjoy sweets, it's just I know it's healthier to stay clear of them."

While she cut the cake and spooned the berries, he offered to refill their coffee cups.

"You know, we've prayed about the bed-and-breakfast, my son's family, and your daughter, but not about our relationship," he said, while adding cream to both cups.

Paula dropped the cake knife.

"I didn't mean to upset you," Rick said, picking the knife up off the floor. "Are you nervous?"

"Sort of, but you're right." She carried the dessert plates to the table, and he brought the coffee.

Silence permeated the dining room.

"Paula," Rick began, "we've only known each other for a short while, but it's been long enough for me to feel God put us together for a reason."

Paula took a deep breath. "I've been thinking the same thing."

He chuckled. "I've been feeling like a kid again."

Paula popped a bit of angel food cake in her mouth. Her heart beat like a hummingbird in flight. She had to keep her hands busy before Rick saw how very nervous she felt. She swallowed hard and choked. Between the coughing and sputtering, Paula reached for her coffee and burned her tongue. Instantly Rick handed her a glass of water.

"Thank you," she finally said. "I'm so embarrassed. Imagine choking on angel food cake."

"Are you sure it was the cake or our conversation?" Rick asked, leaning over her.

"I believe the conversation," she said truthfully, blinking back the tears from the choking episode. "I'm scared, Rick.

This thing between us shakes me down to my toes."

He hesitated and seated himself. "Paula, don't you think I'm scared? I'm the last one who would want to rush into anything. We should take it slow and easy. I'm confident God wants us together, but we need to know each other better. There is a ton of things about me you don't know, and there are even more things I want to learn about you."

Paula reached for Rick's hand. She liked the feel of it, firm and strong. He'd worked hard to build his contracting company, and she knew behind every callus stood a story. On the contrary, John's hands had been smooth. He had spent his working years behind a corporate desk accruing oil leases and expanding his business to one of the top companies in its field.

"I never thought I wanted to care for a man, again," Paula said. "And as long as you understand how difficult it is for me to admit more than a friendship, I. . .well, I'd like to continue seeing you."

Rick's eyes were soft, reminding Paula of a blue cloudless sky. She squeezed his hand lightly and waited for him to reply.

"I believe we're both feeling the same mixed emotions. Believe me, once I moved past the grieving stage when Olivia died, I never wanted to fall in love again. But lately things have changed. You're a fine woman, Paula Franklin, and I am honored to be your friend. What do you say we give our fears to the Lord and let Him work everything out?"

Paula nodded. "I'm ready to pray."

Rick's rich voice echoed in the stillness of the room. "Heavenly Father, we come to You now unsure of the plans You hold for both of us. You've given Paula and me a special friendship, and we sense our relationship is supposed to go further. We're confused and a bit scared about the future. We give it all to You, Lord. We are trusting You to answer our prayers. In Your precious Son's name, Amen."

Paula hesitated before speaking. "Rick, in my quiet time this morning, God spoke to me about confusion and fear."

He lifted an eyebrow. "And what did you learn?"

"Let me get my Bible so I can read it word for word." She

released his hand and retrieved her Bible from her bedroom. "It's in the first chapter of Joshua, where God instructs Joshua to lead His people into the Promised Land. I can only imagine the confusion and fear he must have felt at the thought of the responsibility presented to him." She quickly found the passage and began to read. "Moses my servant is dead. Now then, you and all these people, get ready to cross the Jordan River into the land I am about to give to them—to the Israelites. I will give you every place where you set your foot, as I promised Moses. Your territory will extend from the desert to Lebanon, and from the great river, the Euphrates—all the Hittite country—to the Great Sea on the west. No one will be able to stand up against you all the days of your life. As I was with Moses, so I will be with you; I will never leave you nor forsake you. Be strong and courageous, because you will lead these people to inherit the land I swore to their forefathers to give them. Be strong and very courageous. Be careful to obey all the law my servant Moses gave you; do not turn from it to the right or to the left, that you may be successful wherever you go. Do not let this Book of the Law depart from your mouth; meditate on it day and night, so that you may be careful to do everything written in it. Then you will be prosperous and successful. Have I not commanded you? Be strong and courageous. Do not be terrified; do not be discouraged, for the Lord your God will be with you wherever you go." Paula closed her Bible. "At first I thought the passage was to encourage me with the bed-and-breakfast, but now I see that it applies to you and I as well."

"Be strong and courageous. Do not be terrified; do not be discouraged, for the Lord your God will be with you wherever you go," Rick repeated and rubbed his chin. "I like that advice."

eight

Paula penciled through the items she'd completed for the day. So much remained to be done before she moved into the farmhouse at the end of the week.

The movers were scheduled to pack her house on Thursday. On Friday they would deliver both her household items and all of the antiques in storage to the farmhouse. With the inherited pieces of furniture, she had enough to fill the bed-and-breakfast without investing money into additional furnishings. Of course there would always be antique shops to strike her fancy and cute crafts stores to tantalize her creativity.

Suddenly she remembered the pair of chestnut geldings she'd recently purchased to pull the carriage and wagon. The animals were scheduled to be delivered the same day as the movers, and she'd forgotten to buy feed! Reaching for the phone, she made a quick call to Rick and solved the problem.

Moving down her list, Paula canceled her utility services in Austin. Each call placed her on hold for nearly fifteen minutes.

Next she gave the church her forwarding address and phone number. Hopefully, she'd find a new church home with little difficulty. Rick recommended the one he attended, and the two belonged to the same denomination.

Midway down her list, Paula saw she needed to put together a shopping list. She and Rick had planned an excursion the next afternoon to a wholesale food center. He insisted his truck could hold more supplies than her sport utility vehicle. She smiled to herself. He was right, and the trip provided another excuse for them to be together.

The next item on her agenda involved finding a part-time cook and maid for the bed-and-breakfast. In the beginning Paula figured she could handle the workload, but the first time that all of the bedrooms were full she'd need help. She dialed the newspaper's classified ad number in Brenham and arranged for a "help wanted" ad to begin the following week.

Moving down to the last item on the list, Paula paused to reflect upon her original plans for her home in Austin. She'd wanted to sell it, but then Barbara had told her about Pastor York and his young family desperately needing to move from their apartment. After contacting the young couple and seeing for herself how cramped they were with two children, Paula prayed for guidance. Financially, she could help them, and she felt God leading her to make her home available for their use. Picking up the phone, she dialed her church.

"Pastor York, please," she requested and waited for him to answer. "Hi, this is Paula Franklin. If you've found the documents to be in order, I wondered if we could get together tomorrow morning and sign the lease-purchase agreement."

"They're perfect, Paula. Let me check my calendar. . .Yes, tomorrow morning is fine, and I know Jill will be free, also."

"Is ten o'clock at the lawyer's office all right?" Paula asked. "I took the liberty of reserving the appointment. As you know, he's an old friend of the family by the name of James Sharp, and he's also a strong Christian."

"Sure. Paula, we really appreciate what you are doing for us. The lease-purchase is an answer to prayer."

Paula laughed. "No, you are an answer to prayer. I didn't have to list the house with a realtor, which saved both of us money. Are the original terms going to work for you?"

"Yes. When will we have possession?"

Paula mentally pictured the happenings over the next few days. "If you can come by early Friday morning before the movers leave, I can give you the keys and you can move in during the weekend. The carpet will be steam cleaned late Friday afternoon, so it should be dry by Saturday."

"Moving in on Monday will be plenty soon enough. With my busy schedule, the weekends are crazy."

"Okay. Then I'll see you and Jill tomorrow at ten o'clock?"

"Right. Thanks for calling; we're looking forward to it."

As soon as Paula hung up the phone, she verified the time

with the lawyer's office. Two more things were marked off her list.

Paula sat down and gave a sigh of relief. Knowing Pastor York and his wife were moving into the house gave her immense peace. She'd agreed to a lease-purchase so the couple could buy the home in six months' time. All of their payments would be credited to the down payment, and she planned to carry the mortgage, if necessary.

Remembering yet one more important matter, she dialed Jill York, the pastor's wife.

"Hi, Jill," Paula greeted. "Has your husband called you yet?"

"Yes, everything is fine, and I'm so excited. And I'm only days away from being ready to move."

"Me, too. I called to let you know that it is fine to change the wallpaper in the bedroom to go with your little boy's decor. And go ahead and stencil the wall in your daughter's room, too. I think it will look great. After all, in less than a year the house will be yours anyway."

"Thanks, Paula. I never dreamed we'd have a home so soon, and we are so grateful. I'm looking forward to tomorrow morning."

"Wonderful. I'll see you then."

Paula hung up the phone and snatched up a cup of coffee and a banana. She'd neglected to eat breakfast, and her stomach growled. She readied herself to begin the next project. Each room in the farmhouse needed to be assigned furnishings. Glancing at the living room floor, she shook her head at the pictures and bits and pieces of fabric strewn everywhere. What a project! And Barbara had promised to help. Together over coffee and later lunch, they'd compile all the notes, arrange furniture placement on graph paper, and organize The Country Charm.

❧

"Barbara, I just remembered an entire set of green Depression glass in storage! There's service for sixteen, plus serving pieces," Paula said excitedly. "I believe there are salt dips, a covered butter dish, a huge sandwich platter, and a vegetable bowl."

"You are one lucky lady to have all of these goodies for the bed-and-breakfast. I'm truly envious."

"Well, you know that most all of my things came from John's side of the family. I used to wonder what in the world I would ever do with some of them, but God obviously had a plan. I even have an old rooster weather vane, and he's quite a charmer."

The two laughed. Barbara took a sip of freshly brewed coffee. "This is not bad for decaf. Why did you decide to switch from leaded to unleaded?"

Paula looked like a little girl just caught with her hands in a cookie jar. "Rick," she said meekly. "He drinks decaf, so I thought I would change, too."

"I think wedding bells are in the future," Barbara said with a nod of her head.

For the first time, Paula didn't deny the possibility. "Maybe," she said. "We haven't known each other very long, but so far everything is. . .very nice."

"Don't elope," Barbara warned. "Wade and I want to be there. By the way, my husband really likes Rick—not that his opinion would sway yours."

"But it is good to know," Paula added, then paused thoughtfully. "We do get along quite nicely."

"Is there anything else you haven't told me about the charming Mr. Davenport?" Barbara grinned.

Paula pretended to ignore her and picked up a file folder. "I can't tell it all, now can I? What would you and I have to talk about?" She giggled and leafed through her notes, then closed them again. "You know, my mind says I'm a kid again, but my body says, 'Paula, you'll soon be fifty.' Why, even this morning I saw a new wrinkle."

"I saw more than two in my mirror! The comforting thought is our men have wrinkles, too. I used to hear my mother say the same thing. She insisted her mind was that of a young girl, she just needed to remind her body!"

Laughter rang throughout the downstairs of Paula's Austin home. She poured them another cup of coffee and seated herself on the floor beside Barbara.

"All right friend, where were we? Oh, the kitchen, pantry, half-bath, back porch, and my bedroom and bath are ready to go."

"What did you decide to do about your bathroom?"

Paula wiggled excitedly. "I found a claw-foot bathtub in excellent condition. It even has brass feet. Then I papered the room with a blue and yellow floral, added a border above the chair rail that has a green background, and papered the lower wall with a blue and yellow check."

"I can't remember the last time I saw you have so much fun," Barbara said.

"And I am. Oh, I found the perfect spot for my spinning wheel in the dining room. There's an alcove just begging to show off something special."

"Are you still planning to hang a quilt on the dining room wall?"

"Absolutely, and I found an oval braided rug to go with it. You would not believe the monster of a black, metal chandelier that Rick pulled out of the attic. I spray painted it forest green. Can't you see my huge oak buffet and table in there?"

Barbara nodded. "I'm amazed at all of the beautiful oak floors and woodwork in the farmhouse."

"Sure glad I didn't try to tackle stripping them myself," Paula said. "Don't concern yourself with the other two down-stairs rooms. I'll worry about them later." She picked up a file folder marked "parlor."

Barbara leaned over her shoulder. "What are you planning for the main parlor?"

Paula pointed all around them. "You're looking at it; all of my furnishings here will fit. The double fireplace between the dining and parlor will be the focal point."

"This isn't as difficult as I thought. Are you ready to tackle the upstairs?" Barbara asked, stuffing pictures and fabric into various file folders.

"Why not? Most of the bedrooms are in order." Paula pulled out the file on the adjoining rooms. "I want this to be a combination parent and child's area done in ivory, country blue, and peach. In the smaller child's room I have a trundle bed and an antique baby bed. I plan to use a Noah's Ark theme in both rooms. The wallpaper and furnishings are already in the file. Oh, I have an old baby buggy filled with stuffed animals for the little ones. Sound okay to you?"

"Sure." Barbara studied the farmhouse plan. "What about this bedroom?"

"Oh that's the Victorian country room. I'm undecided about color schemes. The walls are painted a pale peach, and I have an area rug in black and peach."

Barbara examined the swatches. "What about a strawflower wreath above the bed, maybe an English washstand, your light blue and peach stenciled pie safe, and the carved headboard bed from Kristi's room?"

"I knew I had you here for a reason, and this particular room has two stained glass windows on either side of where the bed will be placed," Paula said thoughtfully. She picked up another folder. "The next room is easy and fun. It's all memorabilia about Stephen F. Austin and history things surrounding Washington County and Brenham. Then I have a Texas room where I'll display John's old sword and gun collection. The stories surrounding the area are rich, and the advertisement agency wants to feature both of these rooms in a brochure. The last bedroom is a dormer."

"Oh, I like this," Barbara admired. "A white iron wedding band bed with all those colors of rose, yellow, blue, and green. It's really airy and a step back in time."

"I like that room, too. I've got a yellow and white pieced quilt to throw over the trunk at the foot of the bed," Paula added. "And I'm papering every bit of it—ceiling and all."

"We're done!" Barbara exclaimed.

"Not quite. The upstairs sitting room needs a little help. I'd like to use stuffed teddy bears, but it needs something else."

"What about a fishing corner? You could mix the bears with all sorts of fishing gear. Add some stuffed chairs and you're all set."

Paula took a deep breath. "Um. . .I like that idea. Okay, you sold me, and now we are really done, which is great because I'm starved. Are you ready for lunch?"

"Yes, and I'll help you." Barbara stood and took an interested glance out of the window. "When was the last time you talked to Kristi?"

Paula tilted her head and considered the question. "I guess when she informed me I owed her a financial future. Why?"

"Well, she just pulled into the driveway."

nine

Paula and Barbara watched Kristi emerge from her car. The young woman looked impeccably dressed in a navy blue suit and matching pumps. Paula saw the stubborn set of her jaw. How many times had she seen that look in her father? The big difference between father and daughter lay in their convictions about God. Never had Paula dreaded a discussion with John Franklin. Even when the two were angry, they based their communication upon the Lord.

"I have no idea what she wants," Paula murmured. "But from the look on her face, I'm afraid to ask."

"I'm praying for you," Barbara said, reaching up to place a comforting hand on Paula's shoulder. "And I'm not leaving, unless you ask me."

"Trust me, I won't be asking you."

The doorbell chimed and with a determined look of her own, Paula opened the door.

"Hi, sweetheart. It's so nice of you to stop by." Paula forced her voice to sound light and cheery. She reached up to give Kristi a hug, but the young woman stepped back.

"I'm in no mood for displays of affection," Kristi said, devoid of emotion. She walked inside and noticed Barbara in the foyer.

"It's good to see you, Kristi," Barbara smiled. "It's been a long time."

Kristi nodded cordially and turned her attention to Paula. "Mother, may we have some privacy?"

"I think whatever we have to say can surely be said in front of Barbara," Paula said pleasantly.

"This is a family matter of utmost importance, not a sweet chat among friends," Kristi said coldly, but Paula wouldn't hear of it.

"I guess it doesn't matter," Kristi began with a sigh. "I just wanted to verify a particular concern."

"Would you like to have lunch with us while we talk?" Paula asked.

"No thanks. I need to get back to work, so I'll get right to the point. A few minutes ago I was at the bank and ran into Jill York. She told me that you had made this house available for her and the pastor. In fact, they plan to move in on Monday."

Paula smiled. "Yes, I did. They've been wanting to purchase a home for a long time."

Kristi tapped her foot against the tile floor and crossed her arms. "Mother, why didn't you ask me if I wanted the house?"

Paula immediately felt guilty. "I'm sorry. Frankly, I didn't think."

"Didn't think? Is this like the broken-down farmhouse investment? I don't recall you did much thinking about the expense of that venture, either."

Paula wet her lips and prayed fervently. "I'm sorry you're upset, but you have never indicated a desire to have this house. If I'm not mistaken, you recently purchased a condo."

"I could have leased it," Kristi insisted, her dark eyes blazing.

"And you could have expressed interest in your old home. Kristi, you knew I had bought the farmhouse and remodeled it for my new home. Why didn't you speak up?"

The young woman stared into the calm face of her mother. Paula's control seemed to agitate her even more. "Mother, this is pointless. Once again you have demonstrated inappropriate business judgment. It only serves to prove how incompetent you are in managing your own affairs."

"Kristi, you have said quite enough," Paula said firmly. "I won't tolerate your rudeness. I have nothing more to say about the matter."

Kristi opened her mouth, but thought better of it. She turned and left, leaving the front door open.

Barbara gently closed the door. "Go ahead and cry, Paula," she urged.

Paula shook her head. "No, I don't feel like crying, not right now anyway. Truthfully I feel nothing but pity for my daughter. I can't imagine anyone being so miserable and un-happy over money and possessions, especially someone who once walked with the Lord. It's a good thing John never saw her like this. It would have broken his heart."

"She doesn't even look the same," Barbara said, watching Kristi get into her car.

"I know exactly what you mean." Paula ran her fingers through her hair. "It's as though a dark cloud has settled on her. I remember when her whole face glowed, and when she walked into a room, everyone took notice of her."

Barbara hesitated. "I know she's saved, but the light is gone—the love light of God."

"And she is so miserable," Paula said sadly. "Only He can fill her heart again with joy."

≈

The morning of the move, Barbara and Wade arrived before seven, bringing bagels and cream cheese. Her friends were a welcomed sight. For as excited as she felt about The Country Charm, this had been her home for twenty years and a great deal of sentiment went into every corner. In short, Paula felt overwhelmed.

Nibbling on a banana walnut bagel, Paula watched the movers load the last of her boxes into the truck. A tear rolled down her cheek, and she quickly wiped it away, but not before Wade saw it. Taking a gulp of coffee, she hoped he chose to ignore her.

"Barb cried when we left our old house," he said gently. "I had no idea what brought on the tears and wondered if she regretted building the new home. She said the tears were for the memories that couldn't be recaptured in any other house."

Paula agreed and blew her nose on the napkin intended to whisk off bagel crumbs. She wanted to say the memories of John and a loving daughter lived there, except she knew those words invited buckets of tears. A new life awaited her in Brenham, and she'd always loved an adventure. Rick Davenport was there, and although she felt a twinge of fear about their relationship, she realized God had put them together for something very good.

The words from Joshua 1 came to mind. "I will never leave you nor forsake you. Be strong and courageous." She took a deep breath and swallowed her tears. *This is what I am supposed to do,* she thought with renewed strength. *The past is behind me, and my new life is ready to begin.*

Once the movers locked the truck and Paula had given the house keys to Jill York, she climbed into her car with Tapestry and with a nervous smile led the procession to Brenham. Barbara and Wade drove behind her, and the truck followed. With no one sitting next to her except Tapestry, Paula cried and spilled out her heart to God. Tear after tear fell for John, Kristi, and the old wonderful memories. She believed she acted in obedience to the Lord's command, and she looked forward to every aspect of her new life, but the tears still fell.

The hour and a half drive to Brenham sped by faster than Paula realized. Once she'd dried her eyes, she listened to Christian music. Before long, she was singing at the top of her lungs. Tapestry didn't appear to value her voice, for the cat curled up in the backseat and slept. Soon she found herself looking forward to seeing Rick.

Paula saw several cars parked up and down the road in front of The Country Charm. She expected Rick to be there, but who were the others? As she pulled into the large driveway, Rick waved from the center of a group of people. Her stomach turned flip-flops as he walked toward her wearing a grin as big as Texas.

"Good morning," she greeted, as he opened the car door. "Who are all of these people?"

"My kids and my crew. I wanted to make your moving day as easy as possible. Sure hope you don't mind, but my daughters and daughters-in-law have food for an army, and the men are ready to do whatever is needed."

Paula bit her lip and fought an onslaught of more tears. "Don't mind me, Rick. I've been crying all morning—first leaving the house of twenty years and now with your sweet thoughtfulness. Thank you for thinking of me."

"Are you all right?" he asked, concern creasing his brow.

"Oh yes. This must be one of the most exciting days of my life, and you have made it even more special. Thank you, Rick, thank you for all you've done."

"As long as I can still come around," he grinned, and she saw her reflection in his sparkling blue eyes.

Paula hesitated, then said softly, "Every day, if you want."

"Deal," he said with a clap of his hands "Now let me introduce you to the family." He waved and welcomed Barbara and Wade. "Come on over and I'll introduce y'all to my family."

Paula thought she'd never remember all of the names. Rick had two boys: Andy, who was married to Pat, and Rick Jr., married to Susan; and two girls: Lisa, married to Matt, and Shelly, who was married to Don. She tried to remember the children's names, and that's when she lost track of everyone. One of Rick's daughters suggested name tags and went about tearing off pieces of masking tape for everyone to wear.

Paula knew the workers, but not their wives who had come along. They, too, received masking tape name tags. Some handed her homemade jams or canned vegetables, and others offered to help unpack. She recognized Lupe, the foreman, and he introduced his wife, Irene.

"I understand you are looking for a cook?" Irene asked with a wide smile.

"Yes, I am," Paula said, immediately caught up in the woman's round, brown eyes and petite frame. "Are you interested?"

"Yes, ma'am. I cooked for a Mexican restaurant in San Antonio before we moved to Brenham. Lupe says you want a part-time cook and housekeeper."

Paula nodded. "I just need help with breakfast and housework once we have guests."

"The hours would be perfect for me. Can I come and cook for you a few days without pay? That way we would know if we can work together and if my cooking is satisfactory."

Paula was impressed with the woman's confidence and offer

to cook without pay. Her smile would warm the hearts of many a guest at The Country Charm, and possibly her cooking would bring them back.

"You're too skinny and pretty to be a cook," Paula teased. "But oh, I'd love to give it a try. None of this cooking free nonsense, though; I insist upon paying you. Believe me, you would be an answer to prayer."

The two arranged to meet the middle of the next week. Paula looked around at her new friends. They all had found time in their busy lives to make her feel welcome. No doubt with their help, she'd find the days ahead much easier. One more time, Rick managed to surprise her. Surely God had given her a new family to love.

"We're ready to unload, Mrs. Franklin," one of the movers called. "We'll need to first unload the furniture you had in storage."

Paula cringed. She needed to instruct them where to put everything.

Barbara sensed her emotions. "I know what goes in the upstairs rooms," she said. "Just send them up, and I'll have the things set where we discussed."

"I'll help," two more women announced.

"Wonderful," Paula breathed. "The files are in the backseat of my car. Oh my, I nearly forgot. My cat is back there, too."

"I have coffee and tea made in the kitchen," Irene said. "Would you like for me to help in the kitchen?"

Paula nodded and agreed to everyone who offered. She caught a smile from Rick, and he winked. He wound his way to her side.

"You are even more beautiful when you're happy," Rick whispered as they walked toward the moving truck.

"Sometimes I don't think I'll ever stop thanking God for sending you to me," she replied. "You have done everything in your power to make my life wonderful since the day we met."

"Oh, be careful, you'll see my bad side," he warned. "I tend to be a perfectionist."

"I would never have guessed," she said with an ambiguous smile.

"I'm looking forward to seeing you on a regular basis," Rick said. "I'll most likely make a nuisance of myself."

"Not as long as you promise to come every day for breakfast."

"Um, tempting, but I'm a coffee, skim milk, and cereal man," he added. "Country breakfasts are great for some folks, but not me."

Paula looked surprised.

"I'll tell you about it sometime," he said with his familiar grin. "Look over there. Do you see anything out of the ordinary?"

She followed his gaze to the newly constructed barn. One of his crew had just led a pair of chestnut mares into her view. "Oh, the horses are here, and you've taken care of them for me."

"Just this once," he teased. "I'll come by in the morning and show you how to groom and feed them. By the way, what are their names?"

"Floyd and Boyd."

They heard voices behind them. "Dad, Paula, you two can do your courtin' later. Right now there's work to be done!"

"Isn't that like a bunch of kids?" Rick declared. "Oh, well, guess we'd better get busy." He turned to Paula and burst into laughter.

"What's so funny?" Paula asked, knowing full well that she'd turned beet red at the group's teasing.

"You are precious. . .my blushing country girl."

ten

By early evening all the workers had left for home except Rick. Paula thanked each one for their contribution and invited them back for a barbecue the following Friday night. She felt exhausted, excited, and overwhelmed at the work ahead. Even with the boxes unloaded and the rooms in basic order, she still had many things to do before opening the bed-and-breakfast.

"Honey, you don't have to put everything in its place tonight," Rick said, leading her to a sofa in the parlor. "There's always tomorrow and the next day."

"I need your expertise to organize me," Paula wearily admitted. "I'm going from one thing to the next like a flighty bird, and nothing is completely finished."

Rick produced his clipboard with lots of paper. "Okay, you stay seated and let's start listing all the things you think you have to do."

Paula tucked her feet up under her and closed her eyes. Tapestry jumped into her lap and purred softly. "My mind is spinning so fast; I don't know where to begin."

"You just tell me, then we'll prioritize it later."

"All right. Let's see. . .the kitchen is put together, but I need to grocery shop. My bath is in good shape, and I need a shower. Some sweet lady made my bed. If I knew who did it, I'd kiss her."

"Oh, I made the bed," Rick grinned. "And I'd be happy to accept the kiss."

Surprised, she opened her eyes. "I think I walked into that one," she laughed. "Oh my, all those rooms need wallpaper and two rooms need stenciling. I need to get my web site and my brochure ready. Then there's the decision about what day to be closed—probably Monday. I've got to find a good devotional for my guests. There are boxes of room accessories, pictures, silk and straw flowers—"

"Hold on, girl. Do you have a deadline on all of this?"

Paula tilted her head reflectively. "Only self-imposed," she said meekly. "I really want to open for guests in a month."

"Let's make it two, and do you have anyone to help?" Rick set the clipboard on a cherry table and gave her his complete attention.

"Well, Barbara and Irene offered," Paula said thoughtfully. "I guess it is a little foolish to want to do it all myself."

"Exactly, my point," Rick chuckled. "I sure am glad you tolerate my bossiness. Seriously, don't ever hold back from letting me have it when I get out of line. I've given orders most of my life, so now and then I need to be knocked down a peg. And if you don't do it, I'll just get worse."

"I haven't found your bossiness offensive," Paula said. "But I promise to tell you about it the moment I feel my Irish temper heating up."

Rick slipped in beside her on the sofa. "Can I cuddle up with my best girl for a few minutes before heading home?"

"You bet," Paula breathed, leaning her head on his shoulder. "If you ever buy a place that needs fixin' up, I promise to help. I'll even bring you surprises."

"Like a spinning wheel?" he said softly.

"No—can't have my spinning wheel; it would have to be something else."

Rick squeezed her shoulder lightly. "Will you be up for church on Sunday?"

"Yes, sir. What time is the service?"

"I usually go at eight. Do you want to meet me there? The church is probably not as big as the one you belong to in Austin, but our preacher does a good job."

"What kind of preaching?" Paula asked, enjoying the feel of his arms around her.

"Open Bible, no stepping around the Gospel—not fire and brimstone, but good old-fashioned preaching."

"Um, sounds wonderful. Better tell me again tomorrow

what time I need to be ready, 'cause if you tell me tonight I'll forget it."

If Paula had sat curled up next to Rick for any length of time, she would have fallen asleep. He must have sensed her weariness, for in less than fifteen minutes he kissed her cheek and reminded her to lock up. She roused herself long enough to follow him to the door and then headed to the bathroom.

Wow, a shower in my very own bed-and-breakfast, she thought sleepily. *And tomorrow I'll wake up in the house of my dreams.*

Finally Paula climbed into bed. With the fragrant smell of rose potpourri filling her nostrils and the fresh feel of new sheets, she attempted to sort out the day. New and old friends had made her move easier, and she felt so grateful. She wanted to dwell on what each one had done for her, but her eyes refused to stay open. Whatever would she have done without Barbara, Wade, Rick, and all of the others? Smiling in the darkness, she thought how God had truly blessed her. She'd accomplished a great deal for a widow who had spent the better part of the last five years grieving. Again she had purpose and meaning. No more fighting to climb out of a well of depression. God had seen her through the worst of times.

Paula laughed in the darkness. So Rick did have a few faults after all! He not only confessed to being a perfectionist, but he also admitted to being bossy. Good. She hated to think he might be near perfect.

Suddenly Paula thought of Kristi. She wished her daughter had been there to share the day. Even more, how she longed for the two of them to have a close relationship like they once shared. Paula had given the matter over to God only to take it back again. *Lord, only You can restore my daughter,* she prayed. *I know I'm here for a reason, and I haven't a clue as to why. Perhaps You need Kristi alone to work on her, or You need me alone to work on my life. Whatever Your plan, use me. Let me glorify You in everything I do. Amen.*

❧

Several weeks later found Paula deeply engrossed in a craft

project in the backyard.

"Paula, what on earth are you doing to that milk can?" Irene asked from the back porch.

"Fixin' it up," Paula called to her new friend. "Come and take a look; I need an opinion."

With perspiration streaming down her face, Paula watched Irene walk toward her. It amazed her how close she and Irene had become in a matter of a few weeks. Paula wiped the wetness from her nose, but in doing so, she spread lemon yellow paint across it.

Irene broke into a musical laughter and pointed to Paula's nose. "It looks like war paint," she pointed out, "or maybe sunblock. Why are you painting in the hot sun?"

"Oh, Irene, I'm so impetuous. Sometimes when I get an idea, I don't think any farther than the end of my nose. This project would have been much easier in the shade."

Irene peered at the nearly yellow milk can. "We could pull the drop cloth under a tree."

Together they managed to tug the can into a cooler area.

"Why yellow?" Irene asked once Paula stood back to scrutinize her project.

She scratched her head. "Oh great, now I bet I have paint in my hair."

Irene nodded, and they both laughed.

"Oh well, you asked about this masterpiece. Yes, I'm painting it yellow and then I plan to stencil a purple cow on the side," Paula stated.

"Purple?"

"Yes." Paula saw a thin spot where the previous color of black still showed through, and she lightly brushed a layer of yellow. "Do you remember the nursery rhyme about a purple cow?"

Irene thought for a moment. "How's that go. . .I never saw a purple cow, I never hope to see one, but I can tell you this right now I'd rather see than be one?"

"Yeah, you've got it. I thought it would be a cute addition to the front porch."

"Um, well the purple and yellow will match your pansy theme. And you do have those two purple wicker chairs."

Paula looked at Irene seriously. "Do you think I've gone too far?"

Irene placed her hand over her mouth, and Paula saw she stifled a laugh.

"Don't you know not to hinder an artist at work?" she demanded, trying hard to hold a straight face.

"Oh, no, not me. You just create purple cows all you want. I'm sure the photographer from the bed-and-breakfast directory will love it."

Paula sighed. "He's coming next week, once the landscapers are finished. I might have to hide it."

"Now, now, it's unique and creative. Why don't you take a lemonade break while it's drying and have some warm ginger cookies?" Irene suggested, her eyes big and bright.

"Wonderful. We're going to have to open soon, or I am going to be big as a cow."

"Not as hard as you work. When do you think we'll open?" Irene asked.

Paula paused, considering the question. "The papering is finished, but I have a few extras to add here and there. I still haven't decided on a devotional, yet, and I need to purchase enough Bibles for each room. Can you believe we've accomplished all this in seven weeks? I think the ads for the magazines and brochures go out on Friday and the web site is ready. Don't be angry with me, Irene, but I scheduled our grand opening in three weeks without consulting you first. I'm sorry, I took you for granted, and I never intended to do that. Please tell me if the date is okay."

"The date is fine," Irene assured her. "And while we're taking a break, let's talk about food and decorations for the grand opening."

Paula had quickly learned to love Irene. Down-to-earth best described the pretty lady, along with sensible, reliable. . .and she had a tremendous source of energy. Irene's cooking was matchless. Her husband swore she could take a handful of dirt and make it taste like the best meal in Texas. Paula thought he made a grand analysis, because Irene's culinary skills would certainly help make The Country Charm a success.

Paula remembered a matter of utmost importance. "Irene, we need to talk about church schedules."

Irene nodded and the two headed for the cool temperatures of the house.

Over cookies and lemonade, Irene and Paula worked out the details of attending church and minding the guests. Irene preferred the first worship service with her family, and Paula enjoyed the second. Country Charm guests were scheduled to check out at the same time the second worship service began, so Irene offered to stop by on her way home and relieve Paula for church.

Late in the afternoon Paula dressed for an evening at Shelly and Don's house. She hadn't been anywhere but the bed-and-breakfast, except for an occasional lunch in Brenham, and she looked forward to dinner and the visit.

Choosing a brown and gold sundress, which enhanced her auburn hair, Paula slipped into a pair of gold sandals. Just as she finished adding the final touches to her makeup, the doorbell rang. She took a last minute peek at herself before hurrying to meet Rick.

All the way to the door, Paula told herself to calm down, but lately Rick seemed to have a pronounced effect on her. She trembled whenever he pulled into the driveway, and her stomach turned somersaults at the mere sight of him. Already she felt her pulse quicken and a strange tingling in the pit of her stomach. Paula couldn't tell him what her heart echoed each time that they met. She'd fallen in love with Rick Davenport, and it frightened her to death.

"My, but don't you look nice," Rick complimented moments later.

"Thank you," Paula said with a smile. She dropped the house keys into her purse and willed her heart to slow down. "I'm really looking forward to tonight. In fact, Shelly called this afternoon and told me how much she wanted me to come."

"She's a good daughter," he replied, then chuckled. "Even if she does pester me with taking good care of myself."

"Well I, for one, am glad she does," Paula declared. He squeezed her hand lightly and they walked hand in hand to his truck.

Moments later the two approached Shelly and Don's home. Paula noted happily that the couple lived only a mile from The Country Charm.

"This is beautiful," Paula murmured as they drove into the circular driveway of a fairly new Victorian style home. "Did you build it for them?"

Rick nodded. "Sure did, but Shelly designed it and the horse stables. She and Don did a good bit of the work." He laughed. "Right in the middle of it all, she got pregnant. We didn't let her do any heavy work, but she sure could tell us what to do!"

"Ah yes, I remember my temperament carrying Kristi. I either cried all day or complained. Isn't their little boy named Benjamin?"

"Yes, Richard Benjamin," Rick said proudly. "And the baby girl is Olivia Susan. We call her Livy."

Paula closed her eyes and mentally rehearsed names.

"Don's collie is the one who had puppies," he reminded her. "In fact, he's wanting to give them to some good homes. Are you interested?"

Paula immediately became excited at the prospect of a puppy. "Are they weaned?"

"Yes, ma'am. All you have to do is pick one of 'em out."

She clapped her hands at the prospect of a dog. "Oh, Rick, I'd love a puppy."

Once inside the home, Paula quickly relaxed in Don and Shelly's company. They were the perfect host and hostess, and even Benjamin helped in the dinner preparations. The food tasted splendid with lots of vegetables and a smoked chicken so tender it fell from the bones. They included Paula in all of their conversations and expressed genuine interest in The Country Charm.

Shelly definitely doted on her father. They both had the same crystal blue eyes and gentle mannerisms. Paula liked her and Don immediately. Inwardly, Paula ached for the same sweet relationship with Kristi.

"Why don't we have dessert on the back porch?" Shelly asked, once dinner was over. "We can watch the new colts play in the pasture."

"Sounds wonderful," Paula agreed, "but first let me help you clear the table."

Shelly protested all the while Paula and Rick helped her and Don whisk up the dinner dishes and put the kitchen in order.

"What's for dessert?" Rick asked, accepting a cup of coffee from Don.

"Umm, Dad," Shelly teased. "I think it's strawberry angel food cake."

Rick shook his head and pretended to give his daughter a disapproving look. "Paula, what am I going to do with this daughter of mine? She knows that's my favorite dessert."

"I think you'll have to take a large slice," Paula laughed and caught his gaze. A shiver washed over her, and she instantly turned her attention to Shelly.

"You two are the guests tonight," Shelly insisted. "Please go on outside, and Don and I will serve you."

Rick snatched up Paula's hand, and he escorted her to the back porch complete with white rocking chairs and a beautiful view of the horse pasture.

"I caught you blushing in the kitchen," he whispered with a grin.

"Oh no," she moaned. "I hope Shelly or Don didn't notice."

Rick chuckled lightly. "Oh, I'm sure they did," he continued. "Your face looked about the same shade as the tomatoes we had for dinner."

Paula felt horrified and stared at Rick in disbelief.

"There you go again," he teased, picking up her hand, "but I love it. You know," and his voice instantly softened, "all teasing aside, there are so many things about you that I love, and I really want. . ."

Shelly and Don chose to join them before Rick could finish.

Paula could only imagine what he planned to say, and the thought made her feel warm all over again.

The four talked until the sun started to make its slow descent across the western sky. A pleasant breeze reminded them the heat of summer did sometimes have a cooler side. There were still many days left until the cooler temperatures of autumn.

"Your home is so beautiful," Paula complimented.

"Thank you," Don said. "We certainly enjoy it. God has been good to us."

"What did you think of Daddy's place?" Shelly asked.

Paula shrugged her shoulders. "I've never seen it."

"Shame on you, Daddy," Shelly scolded. "She would love your home."

Rick chuckled. "On the way back tonight, I'll drive by."

"No, don't you dare just drive by. Give her a tour. Why you know she'll love it," Shelly insisted.

Rick conceded easily, and Paula wondered, too, why he'd never mentioned his home.

Don ruffled Benjamin's hair. "Are you going to show the puppies to Miss Paula?"

Paula saw the small boy tear up and made it a point to befriend him. "Benjamin, I only want to see the puppies."

"Daddy said you wanted to take one home with you," Benjamin said between sobs.

"Not if you don't want me to," Paula continued. "I wouldn't dream of taking one of your puppies and making you sad."

Don cleaned his son's nose with a napkin. "Now you can show Miss Paula the puppies and not be afraid. But if you change your mind about giving one away, it is all right." He glanced up at Paula. "We have five, and Benjamin can't bear the thought of parting with any of them."

Paula took Benjamin's hand and allowed him to lead her to the stables. The mother collie sniffed at Paula until she felt comfortable, then laid down to watch her brood. The puppies yelped and played while Benjamin and Paula cast admiring glances at them.

"Which one is your favorite?" Paula asked, picking up two

brown and white puppies and plopping them in her lap.

Benjamin pointed to the smallest one. "He's the baby."

Paula smiled warmly while the little boy scooped up his favorite. "All of them are precious, but I'm like you. The baby is the cutest."

Benjamin grinned and snuggled the puppy up against his face.

"Can I come and visit them again?" she asked.

He nodded. "Yes, ma'am, you can come anytime Grandpa will bring you."

Later as Rick and Paula began their good-byes, Benjamin ran off to the stables. No one seemed to know exactly what he had in mind. Moments later he rushed out carrying the smallest puppy.

"Here, Miss Paula," he said breathlessly. "I know you will love him as much as I do."

Paula bent to Benjamin's side. "Are you sure you want to part with your favorite puppy?"

"Yes, ma'am. You're a nice lady, and I know you'll take good care of him."

She gave Benjamin a hug and kissed his cheek. "You come and visit him anytime. Do you have any suggestions for a name?"

He thought for a minute. "I kinda like Harry."

"Me, too. Then his name is Harry."

eleven

Rick's truck slowed for the right turn that headed toward The Country Charm, but instead he swung left. Paula looked up from examining Harry.

"We're going past my country charm," he explained. "It's about time you saw where I live."

"But, Rick, you don't have to," she insisted. "Besides I don't believe you really want to do this."

He stopped the truck in the middle of the road and shifted into neutral. "Why do you say that?" His blue eyes, warm and sincere, captured her gaze.

Paula swallowed and wet her lips before speaking. "To begin with, you never speak of home; it's 'back at the place' or 'down the road.' You're always out and about, and I wonder how much time you actually spend there. Maybe I'm wrong, but I think the memories are too painful."

Rick said nothing, but studied her face for several moments. Paula tried to read him, except his expression remained emotionless.

"I'm sorry, I shouldn't have pried into your affairs," she said, gently stroking the puppy.

"I'm the one who needs to apologize." Rick reached across the seat and placed his hand over hers. "Olivia and I built the house together. In fact, we designed it from all the other homes I'd built. She'd kept a scrapbook for many years filled with special custom features that we liked, similar to what you did with the bed-and-breakfast. We planned to live there until our grandchildren wheeled us out. Shortly after we completed the house, Olivia got sick, so sick that she never got to enjoy it. She died there. I should sell the place and move or let one of the kids have it, but I just keep working and doing nothing about the situation. The place depresses me because I see her in every room. So I live in my office, the kitchen, and my bedroom. The rest of it sits there for the maid to clean.

"Paula, I don't want you to think I've lived here and grieved for the past eight years, because I haven't. Once I got past the first two years, the Lord coated my heart with memories and no regrets." Rick paused. "The truth is, I don't like the place. In fact, I like yours much better. It's filled with hope and laughter, and my dear old grandmother is lurking behind every corner."

His last remark caused Paula to laugh. "Now I understand," she said softly. "Once I worked through my grieving, I still felt uncomfortable living in our old house. My husband's smells lingered in the closets even after I removed his clothes and painted the walls. I pictured him sitting in his recliner and listening to devotions on the radio. I even poured him a cup of coffee a few times because everything seemed so familiar. It was to be a constant reminder of the past, even though I moved ahead into the future. Moving to the farmhouse was one of the best things I ever did for myself."

Rick nodded in agreement. "Well, I need to get myself out of my house. Like I said before, I should sell the place or make it available for one of the kids, but no, I continue to wallow in my misery."

"Would your children object to you selling the home?" Paula asked, thinking of her problem with Kristi.

Rick sighed as though contemplating her words, then glanced at the rearview mirror. "Looks like I need to go somewhere before we get run over." He shifted into first gear and accelerated. "About the kids. . .I don't think they would fully understand because they haven't been in my shoes, but I'd be surprised if they objected."

"Not like my daughter." Paula stroked the puppy and peered out at the road. "Rick, are you still driving to your place?"

"Now, you are calling it the 'place'."

"I thought after what you told me that we should turn around and head back to The Country Charm."

"No, ma'am. It's not dark yet, so you can see my property. Later, I can turn on lights to give you a complete tour. I am proud of the workmanship and design, and you can tell Shelly all about it."

Paula smiled and turned her attention to Harry. He'd curled up into a ball, and the lull of the truck had rocked him to sleep. *You're a strange, wonderful man, Rick Davenport,* she thought fondly. *I see a lot of wisdom and compassion beneath your cowboy exterior. I'm not so sure I deserve your kind attention.*

The truck pulled into a paved, oak-lined driveway that extended back for nearly a quarter of a mile, then circled in front of a sprawling two-story red brick estate. The home curved around the circular driveway with a massive double door entry. As they drove closer, Paula captured a breathtaking view of a stone landscaped pool.

"This is where you live?" she asked incredulously, leaning forward to better see the home.

"Yes, this is where the mail comes." Rick watched her with a trace of humor spreading across his face.

"It's. . .it's beautiful—not just beautiful, but grand. I've passed this on the road to Brenham and often wondered who lived in such elegance."

Rick chuckled. "Are you surprised it's me?"

"Well yes, I mean no."

Rick roared and opened his truck door. "Stay put, I'm going to play tour guide through the homestead. The butler and maid are off today, so I'll have to be on my best behavior." His eyes twinkled with his teasing.

Paula decided to play along. "The cook is off today? Oh dear, I so wanted a spot of tea."

He opened her door and with a sweep of his hand bowed low. "My lady," he greeted, and reached to help her from the truck. She juggled with Harry and attempted to exit gracefully. "Would you settle for a cup of gourmet decaf coffee?" he asked with deep concern.

"Most assuredly, Mr. Davenport. What should I do with my little friend?"

"Oh, just bring him along." A collie emerged from beside the home and headed straight for her master. "This is Sassy;

she's Harry's grandmother. Sassy, meet Miss Paula. I also have a golden retriever named Spurs, but he's out running around somewhere."

"It's a pleasure," Paula replied, allowing the collie to sniff her before giving the animal a pat. She looked up at the impeccable home before her. "This is so grand. I feel like I should be dressed up to see it."

He offered his arm and she linked with his. "Nonsense, you're beautiful as always. Through the front door, ma'am." Rick unlocked the door and ushered her inside.

Paula couldn't remember ever seeing a home so fine, from the polished hardwood floors to the perfectly placed accessories. "Traditional," she murmured. "Oh my, I should have removed my shoes. Goodness, here I am with Harry. What if he. . ."

Rick gathered up the puppy. "I'll hold him until I get a towel. I wouldn't want him to wet on you."

"It isn't me that I'm concerned about; it's your home."

"Everything here cleans up nicely. Let's tour the kitchen first, and I'll get a towel from in there."

Paula felt as though she had been drawn into a magazine picture. Every inch of Rick's home glistened in style, quality, and workmanship. The kitchen spoke of every woman's dream, from the tile floor to the golden warmth of oak cabinetry. The breakfast nook, built into a corner window, was large enough to accommodate all of his children and their families.

"You must be incredibly neat," Paula said, exploring the kitchen. "And this kitchen sparkles with clean and bright."

"Uh, well, the maid came today. Trust me, it looked really bad this morning."

Paula spotted a juicer beside the sink and walked over to examine it. "Do you use this?"

"Sure; I juice everything."

"Oranges and grapefruit?"

"And spinach, kale, carrots, tomatoes, parsley, celery, red and green peppers, whatever I can get in it."

Paula made a sour face. "I know it's supposed to be good for you, but I can't imagine drinking green juice."

Rick laughed. "I'll make one of my specialties for you one day."

"Just don't tell me what I'm drinking," she insisted. "What perked your interest in juicing?"

He shrugged his shoulders. "A lot of things, but mainly I wanted to be as healthy as possible. Have I ever told you what happened to me about three years ago?"

"No, I don't think so."

"It all started—uh oh," Rick suddenly broke off. "Harry just wet on me."

Paula cringed and reached for the puppy. "I'm so sorry; here let me take him while you change."

"No you don't; Harry and I have bonded. I'll get another towel to wrap him in."

"Are you sure? After all, he may do it again."

"Positive," he assured her. "I'll only be a minute."

Silence exploded between them, and she recognized the warm fire blazing in Rick's blue eyes. His gaze sent a shiver up her spine, and she hastily focused her attention on the puppy.

"Are you still afraid of a relationship between us?" he asked softly. With one hand he held the puppy, and with the other he reached around her waist. "We prayed about this, remember?"

Paula nodded and felt her eyes moisten. "You bet; I'm still scared to death."

"Me, too, but I can't deny how I feel."

Paula's heart pounded hard. "I can't deny it, either."

Rick laughed low. "It's a good thing Harry christened me, otherwise I would be kissing you by now."

Paula stroked the puppy. "Guess Harry is my bodyguard," she whispered.

"Well, his strategy worked this time," Rick said as he released her. "Soon as I change, I'll show you the rest of the house." Rick disappeared, leaving Paula deep in thought.

She did want a relationship with Rick. Even so, she had already fallen in love with him. If they were both honest, he most likely felt the same. Who ever thought she could find romance during midlife? She thought this time of her life was supposed to be a crisis. In a way, falling in love with Rick had anchored her deep into a crisis. She definitely had no desire to go anywhere except to establish herself firmly beside him.

I can hear Kristi now, Paula thought to herself. *Rick and I together will give her one more case against me. If she only knew how wonderful he is, then she'd love him, too.*

Rick entered the kitchen wearing a green striped pullover and carrying Harry in a different towel. "Are you ready for the tour? After we've seen the downstairs, we can go upstairs by the staircase here in the kitchen or the double circular one in the foyer."

"Let's start here," she replied and followed Rick to the second floor.

Rick answered Paula's questions about the craftsmanship, the amount of time it took to construct the home, and how much of the work he'd done himself. She loved hearing the pride in his voice. He explained things thoroughly, just like he'd done with the work at The Country Charm. She viewed four bedrooms and four full baths upstairs. On the first floor, he showed her the formal rooms—a library, an office, and a game room not to mention the oversized utility room. It looked as new as the day it was completed.

While Rick brewed coffee, Paula walked through the living and dining areas. Huge arched glass windows extended from the floor to the second story, providing an open, airy look.

"Rick, this is absolutely beautiful," she called to him, admiring the decorative wood trim around the ceilings.

"Thank you, and you've said that before."

"I know, but I'm in awe of your home."

"God's blessed me with things I don't deserve," Rick called.

Paula appeared in the doorway. "We've all been blessed with things we don't deserve." She silently unmasked her feelings for him, feeling safe with the puppy resting in his arms while he made coffee.

"I think you need help," she said, breaking the tension between them. "Let me take Harry."

She gathered up the puppy into her arms while he poured the coffee. Maybe she didn't want a bodyguard after all.

ঌ

Late into the night Paula pondered over her feelings for Rick. With a heavy sigh, she regretted not talking about the growing closeness between them. Even confessing it to herself sent her stomach fluttering.

Rick's house. . . Every time she had passed it, she had pictured some lawyer in a three-piece suit directing business from his estate. Then she'd try to imagine a plush office in Brenham suitable for the owner of the home. To learn the owner was her own, precious Rick amused her. *And Kristi thought he looked like a gold digger.*

Paula realized her relationship with Kristi stopped her from moving forward with him. She felt moved to tears. She detested the strife with her daughter.

Oh, Lord, bring Kristi back to You. For I know when she is walking with You, she and I will mend our past differences. I don't care what it takes, just wrap Your arms around her and help her see You as Lord. Oh heavenly Father, please give me direction with Rick. In Jesus' holy name, Amen.

twelve

Paula woke with a start. *This is the day,* she thought wildly. *This is the day before open house weekend.* She threw off the loose quilt and opened the blinds.

"Simply glorious," she said aloud. Stretching her long arms and legs, Paula anticipated a wild but exciting next three days. If she didn't hurry, Irene would arrive before her shower, and she wanted the fresh nutty aroma of coffee brewing the moment Irene walked in.

"Gotta hurry," she sang in a nondescript tune. "Gotta hurry and make sure The Country Charm is ready and armed for open house."

After a quick shower, a light touch of makeup, and a vigorous brushing of auburn hair, Paula set to work measuring coffee and mentally calculating what needed to be done. As soon as she poured water into the coffee maker, she snatched up paper and pencil to make a list.

The sound of a truck pulling into the driveway caught her attention, and she stole a look as Irene stepped out from the passenger side. Every morning Irene followed the same routine. She walked around to Lupe's side, lingered a moment, and gave him a kiss. Paula shook her head. She felt a little envious of their relationship. The two were genuinely in love with each other as clearly as the first day they married.

"Morning," Irene greeted shortly thereafter. "Um, the coffee smells wonderful."

"Thanks. It's almost ready."

Irene took a second look at Paula's face. "You're flushed, Paula, just like you always are when you're excited."

Paula grinned. "Guilty. Aren't you, well, excited?"

"Absolutely. Especially since we've been ready for nearly a week. Today is the easy stuff." Irene savored the first drink of coffee and peered around Paula. "Oh my, you've started a list. I think you've been around Rick too long."

"Probably so. Do you want to help me?" Paula suddenly remembered Irene's agenda. "Never mind, you're baking all day, and I'd rather have my list than yours."

"I agree," Irene replied. "Just leave me to my kitchen and I'm perfectly content." She lifted the cup to her lips. "This weekend will be a trial run, right?"

Paula nodded.

"So I need four pots of coffee upstairs, decaf and regular, then a flavored decaf and regular. Then we want regular hot tea and a decaf herbal blend."

"Yes, ma'am. Would you mind baking some miniature muffins to set beside them?"

Irene laughed. "I already have muffins on my list." And she produced a piece of paper from her purse.

Paula gave her a wry look before refilling her coffee. "And what else is Miss Irene baking today? I might need to do a taste test."

"Apple, blueberry, lemon poppy seed, chocolate, and cranberry orange muffins," Irene began. "I'd like to whip up a carrot cake, brownies, oatmeal raisin cookies, chocolate chip cookies, and gather up the fruit for the trays."

"You'll still be baking when we open," Paula accused, but she already knew how fast Irene worked and the delicious results.

"You run on and get your things done, 'cause I can't bake a thing with your fingers in the dough." Irene shooed her out of the kitchen, list and all.

Paula started with the upstairs. She scrutinized each room to make sure it stood ready for potential guests. A Bible and a notepad with a picture of The Country Charm rested beside each bed along with a devotional. She noted ink pens missing from the nightstand and scribbled "pens" on her list. A thorough check of the bathrooms revealed fresh towels and small pastel soaps in the shapes of angels, Texas, tiny arks, and Victorian ladies.

In the second floor sitting room, different types of devotionals for adults, teens, and children rested in a goat cart along with Christian fiction and nonfiction books for leisure reading. An assortment of magazines lay on an old trunk used as a sofa or small game table. Paula wrote "turn on music" on her list. She checked the individual heating and air-conditioning controls in each of the rooms and the intercom system with a music option. Satisfied with the rooms' appearances, she headed downstairs to retrieve the pens. The old steps creaked with age, but she loved it. The sound reminded her of the countless stories Rick had told about his childhood.

Irene accused Paula of playing the part of a detective as she slowly inspected each room. A picture needed a slight adjustment, and she moved a vase of silk flowers three times until she let it alone in its original spot.

"Irene, how do you think the guests will feel about Tapestry?" she asked, standing in the doorway of the kitchen. Tantalizing smells poured from the room.

"I don't see your cat very often. I think it prefers your room to people."

"That's true," Paula replied. "Unless someone complains or has an allergy, I'll not change anything."

"Now Harry is another matter," Irene laughed. "It's a good thing he's confined to the kitchen. He'd want to sleep with the guests."

"Oh, he's going to be my bodyguard," Paula informed her.

"Some help he'd be. All he wants to do is eat and play."

Paula reached down and patted the puppy before disappearing into the music room. This room was one of Paula's favorites. A restored player piano and an old Victrola complete with a few original records guaranteed to be a hit, but she also selected a cherry upright piano for the guest musicians.

The warm colors of the library provided a cozy atmosphere. She'd placed a couple of afghans there to curl up with when sleep escaped the guests. The books were a mixture of past and present on subjects from collecting dolls to playing football.

Finally the parlor and dining room fell under her critical eye.

It took only a few more moments for Paula to realize the interior of The Country Charm readily awaited guests.

"I'm heading outside," she called to Irene. "Do you mind catching the phone for me?"

"Sure. Do you want me to take messages?" Irene asked.

"Yes, please. Holler for me if you need to."

Paula couldn't have asked for a more perfect day. She didn't see a cloud in the sky, and the temperatures rested in the mid-eighties. Glancing around, she fixed her gaze upon the sign advertising The Country Charm. A freelance artist from Brenham had designed it as a replica of her bed-and-breakfast. Below the painting were the words: "Come with me by yourselves to a quiet place and get some rest. Mark 6:31."

She walked to the road and turned to scrutinize the front porch. It looked country cheery, just as she originally envisioned. Even the yellow milk can with the purple cow appealed to her. Amidst the front flower beds she'd placed an old fence post with a yellow enameled pan nailed to the top. She grinned at an iron silhouette of a black bird bent low for a drink and a lopsided sign that read "baths 5 cents." Walking on around the house, bits and pieces of whimsical country accents caught her eye. In one spot she had placed a red paint-chipped chair with a bit of grapevine wound around the top and a sign that read "bird-watching chair." Paula stopped and admired the gazebo. It looked simply romantic and inviting.

Baby animals for the children to pet frolicked in the fenced pasture, and the horses stood groomed for the carriage and hayride events. She'd hired a man to train and take care of the animals, a retired bronco rider by the name of Keifer. He'd found the Lord during his rodeo days and had been singing His praises ever since. Keifer was a pencil-thin, balding man who loved horses and singing old gospel hymns. Of course, Rick had found him for her.

She paused for a moment to thank God for making the weekend possible.

You are so good, Lord. You have made this all happen, and I'm so grateful.

The Country Charm bustled with activity. Young and old toured the bed-and-breakfast, sampled Irene's goodies, and strolled through the grounds. Keifer kept Floyd and Boyd busy with carriage rides, and his historical knowledge of Washington County, plus a keen sense of humor, thoroughly entertained the passengers.

Paula encouraged everyone to sign the guest register. She intended to follow up with a note of appreciation to each visitor. A check on Irene surprised Paula, for her friend couldn't stop smiling. A quick hug and both women were once more busy. Rick arrived shortly before noon.

"This is a great turnout," he said, his eyes trailing over the crowd. "What can I do to help?"

Paula looked around her. "Rick, I haven't been able to fill a single balloon. Would you mind doing it for me?"

"Of course not. I believe I saw the helium tank sitting outside."

Paula nodded and whispered. "These people are making reservations. I'm nearly filled up to Labor Day, and a few families have reserved rooms for the holidays."

"That's my girl," he encouraged, and she caught the light shining off of his silver hair.

"You are a saint," she murmured, but turned her head to his reply, knowing full well she'd blush red. A gentleman caught her attention.

"Mrs. Franklin, I'm thoroughly impressed with your gun and sword collection in the Texas room. My wife and I would like to book the room for two nights during the Fourth of July celebration," he said.

"Oh, but I wanted to stay in the Victorian room; you know, the one in peach, black, and pale blue," his wife said wistfully.

Paula remembered another reservation on the Fourth of July and checked her calendar for availability. "I'm sorry, but the Victorian room is already taken for the Fourth."

"Oh, I'm sorry," the man said to his wife. "Honey, we'll

have to come back another time." She gave him a demure smile, and he promptly reserved the Victorian room during October.

Paula took the couple's information and secured the room with their credit card.

"Thank you so much. I'm looking forward to having you stay with us," Paula stated genuinely.

Someone tapped Paula on the shoulder. She turned and saw Barbara and Wade. The two women laughed and hugged.

"I'm so glad you two are here. God is so good; everyone seems to like the bed-and-breakfast." Paula could barely contain her joy. "And I'm filling up, too."

"I knew you could do it, Paula," Barbara said excitedly. "I know I'm biased, but this is the finest bed-and-breakfast I've ever seen."

"Rick gets the credit for the excellent workmanship. I'd have been lost without him."

"I see you have him hard at work," Wade chuckled. "He offered me a balloon, but I refused." He leaned in closer to Paula. "How's the romance going?"

Paula felt herself redden.

"Aw, no need to answer," Wade teased. "I asked him the same thing, and he just kept filling up those balloons."

"Goodness, Wade, you'll run him off," Barbara pointed out and poked her husband in the ribs.

He sniffed the air, pretending to ignore his wife. "I detect coffee and chocolate chip cookies. Excuse me while I try some of Irene's wares."

"How is Irene working out?" Barbara asked, once her husband disappeared.

"Barbara, she's a gem. I'm not kidding. She can take a can of beans and make a Thanksgiving feast."

Barbara paused and looked around at the happy crowd. "Everything has worked out for the best, hasn't it?"

"Yes it has, all except Kristi." Paula hesitated. "I haven't heard from her since the day before I moved."

"Well, don't give up. One of these days she'll realize the

mistakes she's made and then Miss Kristi will be making a beeline for your door," Barbara said softly.

"You know, Barb, I made mistakes, too," Paula stated softly. "It's partly my fault that she's angry and bitter. I didn't force the issue of counseling when John died, but the only thing I can do about it now is pray. Believe me, if Rick hadn't been around, I would have gone crazy worrying about her."

"No need to ask how your relationship is progressing because I can see it in your face," Barbara said knowingly.

Paula could only smile and nod.

The crowd began to dwindle by four o'clock, and by five o'clock all of the visitors had left. Only Wade and Barbara, Lupe and Irene, and Rick remained. Sitting in the parlor with her friends, Paula couldn't remember ever feeling so tired and so happy at the same time. She stroked Tapestry with one hand and Harry with the other.

"How do you get a cat and a dog to be friends?" Wade asked curiously.

"I keep telling Harry he's a cat," Paula replied, feeling the urge to tease. "I feed him cat food, show him the litter box, and encourage him to meow instead of bark."

The others roared and Wade shook his head. "Guess I asked for that one. Thought you might have a suggestion for our not-so-friendly cat and dog."

"No, I'm just lucky." Paula stopped stroking Tapestry long enough to reach for Irene's hand beside her. "I know I've said this before, but, Irene, I appreciate you so much. None of this could have happened today without your help."

"Thank you, but I'm just a little piece in the puzzle," Irene insisted.

Paula turned to Lupe. "And I will forever be indebted to you for introducing me to your wife."

"Ah, but my Irene can cook." Lupe smiled, patting his stomach. "If Rick didn't keep me busy, I'd weigh three hundred pounds."

Wade picked up a scrapbook from the sofa table. "Hey, I never saw these before and after pictures."

Barbara and Irene chimed in as they all viewed the renovation of The Country Charm. The laughter rose and fell until twilight faded into pink and purple hues.

"I have a suggestion," Rick began. "It's after suppertime. Why don't we celebrate today by heading into Brenham for barbecue?"

Everyone agreed and within moments the group was on the road. Paula felt her mouth had curved forever in a smile, but she couldn't help it. Next week, The Country Charm would be officially open. Already three of the rooms were booked for Friday and four for Saturday.

God is so good, she thought. *Thank You for blessing me with friends and The Country Charm.*

thirteen

Floyd nuzzled up to Paula, his velvety nose searching her hand for a piece of apple. Boyd neighed softly, reminding her of a jealous child begging for one more treat.

"Sorry fellas, but the apples are gone," she laughed softly. Paula drew in a long breath, taking in the sweet smell of fresh hay. She wouldn't trade this life for the biggest house in Austin. Picking up a brush and curry, she began to work through Boyd's mane. For some reason he always had tangles. *Like a little boy who gets his face dirty eating a cracker,* she thought fondly. Keifer did an excellent job grooming the horses, but sometimes she simply enjoyed doing it herself.

Floyd nudged her lightly. "Okay, okay, I'll get to you, too," she laughed. "Our very first guests will not be here until Friday, and already you both are spoiled."

Paula remembered when Kristi used to watch her brush the horses at her father's farm. "Me, too, Mommy," Kristi would say. "I can do it." And Paula would lift the little girl up so she could help. Kristi couldn't wait to tell her father and grandfather.

Paula blinked back the tears. Those days were gone along with her parents, the beautiful, dark-haired little girl, and John, who loved them all.

I'm not going to wallow in self-pity, she scolded herself. *God has been good to me. The blessings He's given me in the past several months are far more than I could ever dream.*

Paula reflected a brief moment more on Kristi. *Oh God, if I only had my little girl back again. Now is the time we could be friends. We could share so many things together.*

When Paula finished grooming Boyd, she stepped around to Floyd. Her thoughts turned to Rick. The mere thought of his name graced her lips with a smile and sent a fluttering to her stomach. His friendship proved priceless, and his commitment to God never ceased to amaze her. Rick's whole being seemed to center on making life content for those around him. Paula wished she could give of herself that unselfishly, with no doubts or fears.

Crystal blue eyes and silver hair etched an image on her heart, and the deep sound of his laughter echoed throughout her waking and sleeping hours. Whatever had she done without him?

I'm in love, she told herself. *I should be open and honest enough to tell Rick all of those things I treasure about our relationship. He certainly has indicated his feelings for me.* But still Paula waited. Admittedly so, her reluctance stemmed from an intense desire to never feel the pain of losing someone again.

Paula finished grooming the horses and stepped out into the sun-washed day to view Harry yapping at a busy squirrel. She shielded her eyes against the bright rays and watched the puppy chase the furry creature around the gazebo. Harry barked helplessly as the squirrel scurried up a pine tree.

The sound of a car pulling into the driveway caught her attention, and she waved at the woman who emerged from it. The visitor carried a large notebook that gave Paula the impression of a potential guest.

"Good morning," Paula greeted, walking toward the car with Harry at her heels.

"Good morning," the woman responded stiffly, not at all friendly like Paula had anticipated.

"Welcome to The Country Charm. How can I help you?" Paula asked. She scooped up the puppy into her arms in case the woman didn't like dogs.

"Are you Paula Franklin?" the woman inquired.

"Yes, I am," Paula responded pleasantly.

"I have papers to serve you," the woman said, producing a large manila envelope.

"Papers?" Paula questioned, slightly taken back. "From whom? For what?"

The woman shook her head. "I only serve these things. I

have no idea of the contents or origin." She opened the car door and drove away, leaving Paula bewildered and confused.

What on earth is this? Paula turned the envelope over and saw it came from a law firm in Austin. Perhaps she had neglected to do something with the bed-and-breakfast, except she had secured both a real estate attorney and accountant who came highly recommended.

Paula walked to the back door. She wanted to give the envelope a toss in the trash, but instead she laid it on the table. After setting Harry on the floor and pouring a glass of iced tea, she stood staring at what remained a mystery. Irene had the day off, and what had once appeared to be a nice, quiet time alone now looked menacing.

"Open it you silly girl," she said aloud.

Paula pulled out the legal papers and began reading. She gasped, then anger ripped through every inch of her. She couldn't believe her eyes! Kristi had filed a lawsuit! Paula exploded into a burst of hot fury. Her own daughter claimed Paula was not mentally capable of handling her own financial affairs! Kristi had sued for control of all her mother's finances.

"Not on your life, little lady!" Paula shouted at the empty kitchen. "Maybe if your dear sweet mother was ninety-nine years old, bedridden, and drawing her last breath, then I might see a little reasoning and logic in this. Kristi Franklin, you don't have a legal leg to stand on, and you have met your match. Some attorney is making a ton of money from your selfishness and greed!"

Harry looked at her curiously, and Tapestry headed for the bedroom. Tightening her grip on the papers, Paula paced the floor. For several moments she recalled the past years of Kristi's bitterness gone rampant. Her mind raced with what discipline she'd like to administer to her rebellious daughter. Turning Kristi across her knee would give Paula an enormous amount of pleasure and satisfaction.

At one point she began to dial Kristi's number, but quickly thought better of it and replaced the phone soundly into its cradle. Paula refused to allow her daughter the satisfaction of knowing how angry she truly felt.

Finally she sat down, and the tears flowed unchecked—angry, pained tears at the betrayal of her own daughter. *Why God?* she asked in confusion. *Why is Kristi doing this? If she truly needed money, I'd have given it to her, but she couldn't possibly need help financially.* Paula knew how much her daughter had inherited from John's estate, and she could live nicely on just the interest. *It simply must be greed,* she surmised. *That's why she wants ultimate control of my finances.* But the realization didn't stop the hurt.

"I've never been so furious," she declared to God. "Of all of the ungrateful, ugly things for a daughter to do, Kristi has topped it!"

Paula felt the need to retrieve her Bible from the bedroom. Tapestry took one look at her and slipped under the bed. Curling up in a chair, she prayed for wisdom, strength, and guidance. *I do love her, Lord, but I'm so angry. Show me what steps I need to take. This is not fair or just, and God, You are a just God. Can't You make this mess right? Must I fight my own daughter?*

As though the passage had been marked, Paula's Bible opened to 1 Corinthians 13. Her eyes trailed to verse four. "Love is patient, love is kind. It does not envy, it does not boast, it is not proud. It is not rude, it is not self-seeking, it is not easily angered, it keeps no record of wrongs. Love does not delight in evil but rejoices with the truth. It always protects, always trusts, always hopes, always perseveres."

"Keeps no record of wrongs and rejoices with the truth," Paula whispered. With tears streaming down her face, she kneeled beside the bed and this time she listened to God instead of demanding justice.

❧

From the library, Paula heard the grandfather clock in the foyer chime six o'clock. Glancing out the window, she saw the sun had begun its gradual descent. It also meant Rick would be stopping by soon, and she really needed his calm and logical reasoning on the lawsuit. She'd spent most of the afternoon on the phone, first with Barbara, then with her attorney from Austin, James Sharp. Both people required details, except Barbara had cried with her.

Paula tucked her long legs underneath her and habitually stroked Tapestry. As of yet, Harry hadn't mastered the art of house-training and was confined to the kitchen much of the time. She heard him yapping and thought seriously of allowing him to curl up beside her, except giving in to his demands failed to help his behavior. The puppy reminded her of Kristi.

Her thoughts continued to replay the conversation with James Sharp. It didn't matter that he was an old family friend, his choice of words seemed cold and formal. Paula felt this incident with Kristi ranked higher than a mere legal matter; it fell under the title of family loyalties. Families simply didn't do these kinds of things to each other.

Her hazel eyes swept over the shelves of books for a particular one to soothe the pain that erupted from her soul. Nothing appealed to her, only the Bible open to the Book of Psalms reassured her of God's immeasurable goodness. She meditated on many of them, especially the ones where David poured out his heart to God over his rebellious son, Absalom.

The distinct sound of Rick's truck aroused Paula's attention. She carefully closed the Bible and took it to her bedroom before heading for the door. She caught a glimpse of herself in the mirror and ran her fingers through her unruly hair.

You look bad today, she told herself. *Put on a smile, girl. Rick will know right away that something is wrong.*

Moments later she poured Rick a tall glass of iced tea with a twist of lemon and a sprig of mint.

"Um," he said after a long drink. "You spoil me."

"Good," she said, wondering when to bring up the lawsuit. "You deserve it. Did you have a good day?"

Rick sat the glass down on the kitchen counter. "Very busy and very profitable, in fact I have an eight o'clock appointment with a couple who wants to build a new home."

"Great."

"Paula."

"Yes."

"What's wrong?"

The moment he questioned her, anger raced through her again. They both sat at the kitchen table while Paula explained the happenings of the day.

"Honey, I'm so sorry. What all did your lawyer say?" Rick asked softly.

"Well, he says Kristi doesn't have a case, but it will still go to court for a judge to decide. Of course, I could give in to her demands, which I won't. Can you imagine her dealing me out a monthly allowance?"

"You don't think she will withdraw the suit?"

Paula shook her head. "I don't know." She saw the color in Rick's cheeks. "You are really upset, aren't you?"

"Guess so," he smiled sadly. "I can't imagine a daughter suing her own mother for money."

"I told God I'd like to strangle her," Paula admitted. "But what Kristi doesn't realize is that I have God's truth and justice on my side. He will fight for me."

"And you claim His word, Paula," Rick insisted. "God has a purpose in all of this, and all we can do is wait and trust in Him." He stood and walked across the kitchen. "So what happens now?"

"I have an appointment with James on Wednesday. I already told him that I refuse to make a settlement."

Rick turned and nodded. "And what do you want me to do for you?"

Paula smiled. "Please sit here next to me." She reached for his strong hand, and her fingertips gently rubbed across one of his many calluses. She loved his hands—so firm and strong. "Would you pray with me?" she asked, staring into his blue eyes. "In spite of all my resolve, I'm still scared."

He grasped both of her hands and bent his head.

"Heavenly Father, we come before You this evening confused and angry at what is happening. We know all things work for good to those who love You. Guide us through this maze of family strife. Kristi needs You, Lord, and we pray for

You to touch her heart and bring her back to You. I pray for Paula to be strengthened with Your peace, and grant her wisdom in handling this suit. All these things we ask in Your precious Son's name. Amen."

"Thank you," Paula whispered. "I wish I could give back to you a small portion of all you've given to me."

Rick reached up and touched her cheek. "I don't know if this is the proper time to say this, but I love you, Paula Franklin. I believe I've loved you since I first set eyes on you."

Paula's heart raced. He'd spoken the words she so longed to hear! "And I care for you, too, Rick Davenport. I thank God for you every day."

fourteen

Paula locked her car and tucked the keys inside her shoulder bag. She immediately felt the intense, stifling heat. No doubt the sun reflecting off the multistory office buildings contributed to the sweltering temperatures. It also sharpened her ruffled emotions about driving to Austin to see a lawyer. With guests arriving on Friday, she had more important things to do.

Taking long strides across the parking lot to the street corner, Paula waited impatiently for the "don't walk" signal to change. Her eyes captured the law firm's sign glimmering in the early morning light. *An expensive building for an expensive lawyer,* she reflected. *Now this* is *a true waste of my money. I can only imagine what Kristi is paying her attorney.*

A trickle of perspiration dripped down her back as she viewed her reflection in the black glass wall of the outer building. Paula looked every bit a professional businesswoman, not a bed-and-breakfast owner from Brenham. Her pale blue suit complete with a white pearl trimmed blouse and a strategically placed scarf set a striking picture against her neatly styled auburn hair. The click of her heels against the pavement reminded Paula of the hot summer day she crossed the same street in the same shoes to read John's will. *What an omen,* she thought.

Inside the crowded office building, the air-conditioning felt delicious, and she tried to bask in the positive things of her life instead of the critical issues before her. *Lord, help me today to use wisdom instead of emotion,* she prayed as her trembling fingers pressed the up arrow for the elevator. The words of Joshua 1 flashed across her mind. "Be strong and courageous. Do not be terrified; do not be discouraged, for the Lord your God will be with you wherever you go." All the while she rode to the twenty-second floor, Paula wanted to ride back down, walk out of the elegant office building, and drive home. Running wouldn't dismiss the problem, though; it might even make it worse.

The familiar surroundings of the law office brought back all the turmoil of John's death: the smell of the wood, the crisp chill, and the strange quietness. Odd, she'd been there only a few months prior with Pastor York and Jill to sign the lease-purchase agreement. After a moment's thought, Paula realized that visit had been under more pleasant circumstances. She'd been full of anticipation about the move to Brenham and her ability to help out the Yorks.

Breathing a quiet prayer, Paula followed the receptionist into a different office than the one where she had listened to John's last will and testament.

"Please sit down, Paula." James rose from his chair to greet her. "Would you like something to drink?"

"No, thank you," she said nervously and set rigid in the plush chair. "I am so glad you agreed to take this case. I'm so glad Kristi didn't contact you to represent her."

James seated himself and shook his head. "Well, it's a good thing she didn't. I think Kristi would have received a piece of my mind. I sincerely appreciate you seeking me out concerning this unfortunate set of circumstances. How is your new life in Brenham?"

Paula smiled. She well understood his need to have her relaxed and calm. "It really agrees with me, James. I haven't been this happy and content since John died."

"Are the Yorks making timely payments?" he asked politely, folding his hands on the desk.

"Oh, yes, over and above the agreed amount."

He took a deep breath. "I guess we need to get started. Do you mind telling me again the whole story behind the lawsuit? You told me on Monday the problems started right after John's death." He took out a legal pad and initiated a few notes.

Paula nodded and retrieved her own pad of paper from her purse. After she relayed the events leading up to the lawsuit, she handed him a file folder.

"Here are the names, addresses, and phone numbers of the accountant and real estate attorney who are handling the bed-and-breakfast. This is my current financial statement, which I had my accountant update yesterday. As you can see, I have not used a quarter of the inheritance for The Country Charm. The second sheet is a copy of my present business status with an outlook projection. The third sheet shows the bookings through the end of the year. This brochure describes my bed-and-breakfast from the physical address to current rates."

James studied the information before him. "Excellent," he murmured. "I believe my wife would love a weekend getaway in Brenham."

She handed him a second brochure. "Good, here is one for her, and it's a free weekend. Now tell me what I can expect from this initial hearing. I see it's set in six weeks."

"The key to all of this is Kristi must show proof that you are mentally incompetent. At the hearing, the judge will review the case and decide whether to throw it out or order a complete psychiatric evaluation."

"And if he does order an evaluation, who pays for it?" Paula felt her anger swell again.

"She does. Now, since you purchased the bed-and-breakfast, have you had any dealings that might lead the judge to question your mental stability?"

Paula piqued at the question. "Absolutely not!"

James smiled. "I have to ask these questions, Paula. It's better you tell me today than for me to be surprised in court."

"I'm sorry," Paula said. "This whole thing has me angry and hurt. In answer to your question, I can't recall a single incident in which I did not use proper judgment."

"Are there any new relationships?"

Paula sat straight up in the chair. "You mean a gentleman friend?" she asked incredulously. The wheels began to turn in her mind.

"Yes, that is what I'm asking. Are you seeing anyone who Kristi would definitely find as a threat to your financial security?"

Paula hesitated. Like a puzzle, it all began to make sense. "Yes, I have a friend. He's the contractor who did all the work for me. We've become very close."

He lifted a fresh sheet of paper and raised his pen to write. "Tell me about this fellow. What has Kristi seen of him, and why might she consider him a threat? Also, I need to know your exact relationship to him."

Paula's eyebrows raised in shock.

"I have to know," James insisted firmly, his gray eyes warm and sincere. "My questioning may not be necessary, but we need to be prepared for the worst."

Paula paused before speaking. It served no purpose to take her frustration out on him. "All right," she sighed. "His name is Rick Davenport, and Kristi met him when she first saw the farmhouse. This was before I bought it. Rick stopped by for permission to give me a bid on the renovation."

"And how did she react?"

"She took him for a gold digger," Paula replied bitterly.

James caught her gaze. "Does she have any just cause to think Mr. Davenport might be after your money?"

"No." Paula wanted to laugh. "The thought is simply preposterous. Rick is a highly influential member of the community. He is wealthy in his own right, but more importantly, he is a Christian."

James nodded while he wrote. "Anything else I should know?"

Paula felt her pulse quicken. "Our relationship is based on a Christian friendship and is totally Christ honoring in every area." She wanted to shout the latter at him. The entire questioning had become ridiculous.

"May I contact him?"

"Of course." She pulled Rick's business card from her purse and pointed out his home, office, and pager numbers. "I despise the thought of dragging him into this," she stated bitterly.

"I understand, but it's better this way. We have no way of knowing what your daughter has planned. Do you want to let him know about my inquiry?"

"By all means," Paula replied firmly. "I'll talk to him today."

"Do you suspect a problem?"

"Most likely not; I just hate the thought of it. What happens after you've talked to Rick?"

"Well, we wait until the hearing. It will be held in Texas State District Civil Court. Frankly, Paula, from what you've told me, Kristi doesn't have a case. Looks to me like she will have spent a lot of money in legal fees for nothing."

Paula sighed. "Oh, I'm sure of it. I have the number one Judge on my side."

In the lobby of the law firm, Paula phoned Rick and explained the meeting and the path forward on the suit. He took the initiative by offering to contact James himself. He felt encouraged by the attorney's counsel, and his optimism heightened her spirits. They prayed together, and she left the building feeling like a huge weight had been lifted from her shoulders.

The visit to James's office hadn't taken nearly as long as she estimated, but she needed time to digest his suggestions before meeting Barbara for lunch.

While waiting inside the Italian restaurant, Paula scanned her notes to make certain she understood everything James had said. She read them twice through and made some of her own observations.

"Hi, girlfriend," Barbara greeted. "Goodness, but don't you look professional."

Paula looked up from her notes and met Barbara's warm smile. "Thanks. I feel more comfortable in jeans or a broomstick skirt and top, but this morning I had a part to play. You look pretty great yourself."

"Thank you. So, how did things go?" Barbara seated herself across from her friend dressed in a long denim sundress.

"Okay. James answered my questions and helped put me at ease." Paula went on to explain what her lawyer had said. "My biggest problem is trying to understand why Kristi feels compelled to file suit against me. I've given up attempting to contact her. Only God can handle my daughter."

"We are praying for both of you. It's a good thing I'm a Christian or I might be guilty of assault and battery," Barbara admitted.

They both giggled and Paula heartily agreed.

"Aside from trying to straighten out the ugly mess with Kristi, are you ready for the weekend?" Barbara asked.

Paula immediately perked. "Oh yes. I'm so excited about my first real guests. You and Wade are still coming on Friday, aren't you?"

Barbara nodded. "My wonderful husband even suggested a little sight-seeing in the afternoon. How many reservations are there?"

"Excellent for both nights. I realize the guests are curious, and it will be my job to make sure they keep coming back. One of the guests on Saturday is a freelance reporter."

"How wonderful, Paula. Is she writing about you?"

"She's putting together an article on bed-and-breakfasts in our area, pictures and everything."

"It's been months in the making, but your Country Charm will be a blessing to a lot of people," Barbara said soberly. "I can feel the Lord in every room. It will be a refuge for those who are hurting as well as those who merely desire a wonderful night away from home."

Paula felt so blessed with Barbara's friendship. She wanted to share all of the many things about her life, especially how Rick had become such an important part of it, but the waiter interrupted her thoughts. After they ordered iced tea with salad and breadsticks, their conversation moved in a different direction. Paula chose not to mention Rick; it was a bit premature.

❧

Once Paula returned from Austin, she and Rick strolled hand in hand through the pecan orchard. He suggested the nut trees should be sprayed for an ample supply of nuts next fall. If the trees were too much work for her, he knew someone who could harvest them. Paula listened intently to Rick's words. She loved the way he explained matters to her. His patience was one of the special things about him that she cherished, along with the stories about his childhood.

"When I was a kid," he began, "we always picked up pecans on Thanksgiving Day. As soon as Grandma cleared the table, Granddaddy would hook up the wagon and off we'd go. Most times we kids ran on ahead and had our buckets half full before he drove up with the wagon. We'd all want to climb the trees to shake them. Of course nobody could shake a pecan tree quite like my dad."

"What did you do with all of them?" Paula asked, glancing up at her own trees.

"Sold them and divided them up between all who helped out with the gathering and shelling. It didn't seem like work because all of us had such a great time."

The two walked past the orchard to a winding creek bordering Paula's property. It felt noticeably cooler beneath the moss-covered trees, which reminded her of huge umbrellas over the rippling water.

"This was my secret hiding place," Rick said, as they threaded their way through the brush. "Whenever I wanted to be alone and think, I'd head straight for the creek. Granddaddy's hunting dog always trailed after me, and I'd pour out my heart to that animal."

"I would have liked to have known you then," Paula said, "unless you were the teasing type."

A chuckle echoed through Rick's hearty voice. "Now, what do you think?"

And they both shared a good laugh. They strolled silently through the field, filling their senses with nature exploding all around them.

"When did you come to know Jesus?" Paula asked softly.

Rick paused a moment and Paula wondered if he might be reflecting upon his salvation experience. "When I turned seventeen, I attended an old-time tent revival," he began. "The Lord spoke to me through this young preacher and convicted me of everything I'd ever done. I will never forget the way Jesus opened my heart and invited me to a relationship with

Him. I cried like a baby. Yes, Jesus saved me from my sins right there, and I was baptized the same evening in the Brazos River. I remember spring hadn't fully come yet, and the water felt like ice."

"Brr. Were there very many baptized that day?" Paula asked, thinking she couldn't have handled the cold water very well.

"Quite a few. My grandma said the cold water was supposed to remind me of Christ's suffering on the cross. She always had a bit of wisdom to pass on to us." Rick pointed to a fallen log. "Let's sit for just a minute. I really enjoy listening to the birds and the sound of the creek."

For the next few moments the two sat silently while nature unfolded around them. Birds called to each other and insects seemed to hold a convention.

"See what I mean," he whispered, leaning into her shoulder.

Paula nodded.

"Now, tell me about your conversion experience."

Paula smiled. "It's not quite as colorful as yours. I was in college and a group of us went to a Campus Crusade for Christ gathering. I had no idea what to expect, but a lot of kids planned to go, so I tagged along. The speaker seemed to be talking straight at me. When he touched on family, peace, purpose, and a God who loved me, I listened. You see, I didn't come from a Christian home. I felt lost and unhappy, and deep inside me I knew something was missing. It took all of my strength to walk down front and accept Jesus, but I managed. Anyway, I've never regretted surrendering my life to the Lord. He's brought me through good times and bad."

Rick picked up a stone and sent it skimming over the water, causing it to ripple in perfect circles. "Do you really think God put us together?" he asked softly.

Paula took a deep breath and felt her stomach flutter. Every time Rick mentioned their relationship, her heart seemed to skip a beat.

"Yes," she finally answered, hearing her voice quiver. "I know He sent you to help me with the bed-and-breakfast, with Kristi, and to give me new joy."

"Anything else?"

"I know you love me, Rick, and I do care for you. It simply scares me to say it out loud. I guess it's because I'm afraid something will happen to destroy it." Paula felt a lump in her throat, and she quickly swallowed to stop any flow of tears.

He brushed a kiss across her forehead. "Don't you think the same thought hasn't crossed my mind? I made a commitment to a special person, too, and when God chose to take her home, I wanted to die with her. He took my grief and covered it with precious memories. He gave me strength and a will to live when my own health failed. Because God carried me through the trials following Olivia's death, I'm a bolder witness and a better person spiritually and physically."

Paula nodded in agreement. "I know exactly what you mean. I had a real problem with God when John died. I felt abandoned. I couldn't eat or sleep, and if it hadn't been for Barbara and Wade and their faithful prayers, I'd have willed myself to die."

"So we both know how it hurts to lose someone we love," Rick continued. He wiped a wispy strand of hair from her eyes. "I'm at the point that I'd rather have you for as long as God allows than to live alone."

Paula felt the tears roll down her cheeks, and she instantly whisked them away. "Rick, I want to be as strong as you, but I'm afraid. I don't know what I'd do without you, and I don't want to think about it. Yet, it seems easier to stop my own emotions than to make a commitment of the heart." She buried her face in her hands. "I'm so sorry. I guess it's the confusion. Sometimes I think my doubts are due to Kristi, and then later I know it has nothing to do with her at all. It's me; I'm a coward."

Rick pulled her to his side and wrapped his arm around her. "I'll keep praying for God to give you a peace and assurance about us. I've prayed about us since the first time we met, and I will keep on."

"You are so patient," she whispered with emotion. "I'll keep praying, too. You are so dear to me, and I don't want to hurt or disappoint you."

"We'll wait this thing out together. As long as you don't mind my evening visits and this face of mine."

"Oh no," Paula interrupted. "You are the highlight of my day. We never run out of things to say, and I love sharing with you."

"Then we'll keep things slow and easy," Rick assured her.

Paula snuggled against his side. She smelled the rich earth around them and felt so secure in his arms. Slowly twilight began to settle in their sanctuary. Their love felt so right, and deep in her heart Paula knew God had brought them together for this special love. Except she'd been through enough valleys and mountaintops in her life to realize the most beautiful of love could have such tragic endings.

"Paula," Rick whispered. "Don't move, but take a look at the creek."

Paula blinked, and her eyes followed the path leading to the creek bank. There a doe drank deeply from the cool water. As if Paula and Rick's eyes held sound, she lifted her head and studied them briefly before bounding off into the thicket.

"A bit of Eden," Paula murmured. "I almost envy her ability to detect danger and take flight." She looked up at Rick and kissed his chin lightly. "But the doe doesn't have you."

fifteen

"Oh my, the first guests are here," Irene said as the doorbell rang the second time. Her huge brown eyes swept over the kitchen.

"Everything is perfect, Irene. Relax; this is going to be fun," Paula said, half running to the front door.

A glance at the grandfather clock in the foyer read five o'clock. Guests were instructed to check in between the hours of four and six o'clock. Once settled in, the guests could leave or explore inside and outside of The Country Charm. Each received a schedule of optional activities including the petting corral, a nature trail, and an eight o'clock hayride that lasted until dark. The latter was Keifer's specialty.

"Welcome," Paula greeted with a big smile. She gestured for a young couple to step inside. "I'm so glad you are here. Come on over to the desk; we'll check you in, and I'll show you to your room."

Moments later, the couple followed her upstairs to the dormer room with the white iron bed.

"Here are your keys, and on the nightstand are items of interest including a devotional and a Bible. Please note the coffee and juice selection for breakfast in the morning. Just complete it and slide it under the door. There is also our brochure with optional activities along with recommended restaurants for dinner." She showed the couple which key opened the front door of The Country Charm and which one unlocked their room. Paula pointed to the intercom. "This dial controls the volume of music. It's the same as played down-stairs and in the gazebo. Bathrobes are located in the closet and fresh linens are in the bathroom. Irene or I are available at all times. Let's see, coffee and tea with chocolate chip and oatmeal raisin cookies are located in the sitting room down the hall. In the morning, coffee will be available in the same room. Breakfast is served at nine o'clock and checkout is at ten-thirty. Do you have any questions?"

"Yes," the stocky young man said. "Are there various sight-seeing attractions listed in the brochure?"

Paula nodded. "More than enough to keep you busy for one evening." She glanced at his wife. "Anything else?" When the woman shook her head, Paula continued, "Then you're on your own until tomorrow at breakfast. I'm sure you will enjoy your stay."

Paula fairly bounded down the stairs. She'd heard the door-bell ring again while visiting with the first couple and she felt anxious to see who else had arrived.

Irene had answered the door, and Paula nearly fell into her friends' arms. "Barbara, Wade, it's so good to see you." She hugged them both, then noted their suitcase. "You could have taken your things on upstairs."

"And miss the official escort?" Wade laughed. "We have the Texas room reserved, Mrs. Franklin. Is it ready?"

"By all means," Paula said with a curtsey. "Only the best for my guests."

"Is the Noah's Ark room reserved tonight?" Barbara asked. "It's so cute."

"Yes, it is. A couple with a toddler have it."

Wade looked alarmed. "Aren't you worried about a toddler with all of your antiques and stuff?"

Paula shook her head. "I do insist that children be supervised at all times, but the Noah's Ark room is set up to accommodate little ones' curious hands."

Wade picked up the suitcase. "Okay, lead the way, and don't forget to give me the complete instructions for the evening."

"Yes, sir," Paula laughed. "Right up these stairs."

By six o'clock the guests had arrived and settled in. All of them elected to take the hayride. Keifer sounded ecstatic. He helped the ladies into the hay-laden wagon and complimented each one on something special. Keifer told his stories about

Washington County and the colorful history surrounding early Texas. Plus he added a little flavor of his own. Once he finished his narrative describing the good old days, he began singing "Texas Our Texas" followed by "The Yellow Rose of Texas" all the while encouraging others to join him. His tenor voice rang throughout the open fields, captivating the guests with his delightful twang.

Paula loved every bit of it, and a part of her heart tugged for Rick to be sitting beside her. If she could only shake the nagging doubt and fear that crept over her each time she thought of losing him. *Where is my faith?* she pondered. If she truly believed God put them together for a reason, then what held her back?

The evening progressed smoothly; even so, Irene and Paula made notes of what they felt could be done more efficiently. Both women agreed the weekend would be a learning experience for them, and together they made adjustments in their schedule to better accommodate guests in the future.

"Look at this breakfast," an elderly man exclaimed the following morning. "It's been years since I've seen a country spread like this!"

"Oh hush," his wife said. "I've fixed you biscuits, gravy, and grits many times."

"Not with scrambled eggs, bacon, sausage, fruit, jam, oatmeal, and blueberry cobbler."

Irene grinned from ear to ear. Paula knew it was just the right thing to say to a nervous cook.

"Do you plan to serve the same breakfast each day?" a lady asked politely.

"Oh, no, ma'am," Irene replied. "We plan to vary every menu, but there will always be large portions."

Paula produced a high chair for the toddler, complete with a tot-size place setting that matched the other dishes. The child's mother visibly expressed her gratitude. Paula gave the blessing, and breakfast progressed smoothly even with the child's father turning over a glass of orange juice.

At checkout time, two couples booked reservations for the

future, and the elderly couple hugged both Paula and Irene. Barbara and Wade made reservations for the following month with a promise to spread the word about The Country Charm.

੨.

As Paula sat with Rick on Monday afternoon telling him all about the first weekend of business, she couldn't help but express her enthusiasm.

"This is my niche," she stated, "my own little ministry right here in Brenham, Texas. Who knows? I might even make a profit someday. No, on second thought, I'd be perfectly satisfied with happy guests."

"I'm glad everything went well," he said warmly. "But I missed you. At least I had your presence in church yesterday morning, even if you did make a mad dash back here."

Paula looked guilty. "I won't need to hurry again. Irene and the guests were gone by the time I arrived home."

"How about a trip to the Blue Bell Country Store for ice cream?" Rick asked. "This weekend is cause for a celebration."

"I thought you didn't care for ice cream," Paula teased.

"I love it; it just isn't healthy for me. Besides, I can get yogurt or something light."

"Well, if you insist; I'd love a dish of strawberries and cream. Really, Rick, I wish I could be as health conscious. I've never met anyone so disciplined."

He squeezed her hand. "Keeps me young, healthy, and one step ahead of a certain redhead I know."

Rick helped Paula lock up The Country Charm and deliver Harry into the utility room until their return.

"Your truck is clean," Paula observed, as they walked toward the vehicle.

"Yeah, I finally got the dirt and mud washed off. In fact, I cleaned it up on Saturday. I had to do something to keep out of trouble."

Paula wrinkled her nose at him. "Well, I did miss you on the hayride," she confessed. "So please don't be a stranger when I have guests."

"Yes, ma'am," Rick said, drawing out the words in a typical

Texan fashion. He started up the engine, and the two headed for Brenham.

The country store was filled with people ordering and eating their favorite flavor of ice cream, yogurt, and sherbet. Since the sun had begun to set, Paula and Rick chose to sit outside in the cooler temperatures.

"Mr. Davenport, you had a marvelous idea of celebrating here," Paula said, dipping a spoon into her ice cream. "How is your fat-free vanilla yogurt?"

Rick grinned. "Wonderful, simply wonderful. I see you are enjoying your strawberries and cream." He waved and greeted a family at a nearby table.

"You must know half the population of Brenham," Paula accused.

"You would, too, if you'd lived here all your life," he laughed. "With your bed-and-breakfast, I'm sure you will be quite the socialite in the community."

They both laughed and talked easily of their fondest childhood memories.

"I fell out of a tree when I was three years old," Rick claimed. "I landed on my head, which is why my mom believed it didn't hurt me."

Paula shook her head in laughter. "Did I ever tell you about the times my grandparents took me fishing?"

"Nope, let's hear it."

"Well, Granddaddy had been trying to teach me how to cast off. So I decided to try it myself and hooked a wasp nest. We all got stung, and it was a long time before Granddaddy let me cast again. When he finally let me go again, I did something just as horrible."

Rick raised an eyebrow.

"I flung the rod back, and this time I hooked his lip."

"Your poor granddaddy," Rick moaned. "Did he ever take you fishing again?"

"Of course. I loved it, and he loved the fact that his granddaughter wanted to hold slimy worms and help him clean fish. You should have seen me in a pair of waders!"

Rick finished his dessert. "I think you and I will have to go fishing. I won't make you clean them, though, as long as you'll cook 'em up."

"Deal," Paula stated. "How about next Monday right after my guests leave?"

Moments later the two headed back to The Country Charm, all the while their bantering bounced back and forth. To Paula, this had become a treasured part of their relationship—fun talk based on wit and teasing.

Rick pounded the steering wheel with the palm of his hand. "Rats," he said.

"What's wrong?" Paula asked.

"Oh, I forgot my medicine. Honey, would you look inside the console and pull out a prescription bottle for me?"

Paula lifted the console and pulled out the bottle. "How many?"

"Just one."

She handed him the tablet and snapped shut the lid. Her eyes followed the instructions on the bottle to the name of the medication.

"This is for your heart," Paula said shakily. She dropped the bottle and hastily picked it up. Again her eyes read the contents. "Rick, tell me this is not for your heart."

"It is for my heart," Rick said softly. "I thought you knew."

"About what?" Paula felt her heart pounding with the implications.

"I had a heart attack a few years ago."

Paula thought she would be sick. "John died of a heart attack," she finally managed.

"I'm not John," Rick said firmly. "And I am in better health than most men half my age."

"But you had a heart attack." Her voice rose and she clenched her fists. "The next time you might not be so lucky."

"Who said there would be a next time?" Rick asked curtly. "After I left the hospital, I lost thirty pounds, started a daily exercise program, and committed to healthy eating. That was nearly three years ago, and all of my checkups are great."

"But you had a heart attack," she repeated.

Rick shot her an astonished look. "What is wrong here? I'm sorry your husband died from a heart attack, but it doesn't mean I will do the same thing." His tone indicated his frustration, and he instantly became quiet. "So this is the problem. You've been afraid to allow me into your life because you're afraid I'll die, and now you find out your husband and I both experienced heart problems."

Paula said nothing. A huge lump settled in her throat, and her stomach churned. The nausea worsened, and when the truck bounced over a hill, she feared vomiting all over herself and Rick's truck.

"I'm sick, Rick," she said simply, "really sick. The ice cream must not have agreed with me."

Rick shot her a quick look. "You are white as a sheet," he noted with a sigh. "But the ice cream isn't what made you ill."

"Probably not. I just need to get home."

He sighed deeply. "I'm sorry, Paula. I never meant to deceive you; in fact I really thought I'd told you."

"How could a heart attack slip your mind?" she demanded.

"I guess I couldn't find the right time to tell you." Rick licked his lips. They rode in silence for the next mile until he spoke. "Remember the night we prayed together at your home in Austin? Remember the Bible passage from Joshua? 'Be strong and courageous. Do not be terrified; do not be discouraged, for the Lord your God will be with you wherever you go.' "

"Please don't quote Scripture," Paula flung at him. "I can recite quite a few on deceit."

"Paula, I didn't. . ."

She turned her head and ignored Rick's plea for understanding. She well recalled the Scripture. Afterward he had prayed for God's direction in their relationship. The budding of new love seemed so right.

When the truck pulled up beside the bed-and-breakfast, Paula quickly exited.

"I'll let myself in," she said, avoiding Rick's eyes.

"Will you call me later?" he asked.

She heard the concern in his voice, but couldn't bring herself to meet his gaze. Bile rose in her throat, and she slammed the door without a reply. Hurrying to the back door of the house, Paula heard him call after her, but she simply couldn't acknowledge him. She felt too sick and miserable.

Devastating news always affected her this way.

An hour later Paula rested on her bed. She'd vomited three times; there couldn't possibly be anything left in her stomach. Between the stomach cramps, the horrid taste in her mouth, and the dull ache in the back of her head, Paula thought death would be a blessing. At least with the life gone from her body, she wouldn't have to think about Rick's health.

The signs of a past health problem with Rick had been evident. Why hadn't she paid attention to his salubrious eating habits, the daily exercise, and his comments about a past illness? She thought he referred to poor health due to grieving the death of his wife. How could she have been so blind and stupid? Why hadn't she questioned his medical history?

Paula knew the answer to her own questions. She wanted Rick to be perfect in every way. She didn't want to concern herself with a health problem. In her heart she'd made a commitment to Rick, a pledge of love. Would God expect her to honor it if she didn't have all of the facts? Of course not, she told herself. She'd made a poor decision, but it wasn't too late to walk away from it. Granted, she'd ache for him, but absence would heal the pain. She well remembered the grieving process, the various stages, and the endless time alone.

Paula remembered the pastor's sermon the night before. In his message, he'd given clear directives in making sound decisions. Ignoring her wrenching stomach, she turned toward the nightstand to snap on the light and read her sermon notes. Her eyes didn't want to focus on the small journal inside her Bible, except she felt compelled to find out if her admittance of love for Rick had been a mistake.

1. Beware of snap decisions and quick judgments. These are usually made without consulting God. *Did I pray enough*

through my feelings for Rick?

2. Even those we love can lead us astray. *Hadn't Barbara encouraged my relationship with Rick? But then again, Kristi warned against it.*

3. Be aware of the world's influence. *I've gotten along fine without a man for over five years, and I can continue to do so.*

4. Consult the Bible for sound principles and seek the Lord in prayer. *I thought I had done that very thing.* She moaned.

5. Don't make life-changing decisions when you are confused and upset.

Paula laid the notes aside. The last point stopped her cold from making the same mistake listed in the first point. She closed her eyes and prayed.

Oh God, I'm so scared. I couldn't handle losing someone I loved again. I've already lost John and Kristi. How much more can I take? Help me, Lord. I don't know what to do. My life is twisted and nothing is going right. Kristi wants to declare me incompetent and now this mess with Rick. Make Your will for my life so evident that I know beyond a doubt it is Your plan for me. In Jesus' precious and holy name, Amen.

Paula rushed to the bathroom as the nausea swept over her body. She hadn't been this ill since the night of John's death.

sixteen

Shortly after midnight Paula drifted into a troubled sleep. The nausea disappeared, but her ribs and stomach ached from the vomiting. She found no way to lay comfortably, and her mind continually replayed the conversation with Rick. A keen sense of betrayal prevailed over the long night. When the chirping of blue jays announced morning, she woke again, reliving the memories of the night before.

After a long shower, she kept listening for Irene, but she'd given her the day off. Her friend's company and infinite stores of wisdom might have helped her work through the problem with Rick, but perhaps she shouldn't burden Irene. The dear lady had already heard all about Kristi. Paula considered calling Barbara, but she didn't want to impose upon her, either. Paula already felt embarrassed for the many times she called upon her friends in Austin.

Country Charm guests would arrive in the late afternoon and preparations needed to be made. Paula forced down medication to settle her stomach in hopes that none of the episodes from the evening before recurred. An hour later, she poured herself a glass of clear soda. Fortunately, she began to feel better, except for the inner turmoil surrounding her relationship with Rick.

She sensed a deep longing for God. Only her Lord and Savior could give peace and direction in the heartbreaking revelation of Rick's health. Yet, she must go to Him; God required her to seek Him out. He had the answers, but did she really want to hear His words?

Rick should have told her from the beginning about his heart, not hinting about a previous problem but an upfront admission about it. Paula shivered; guilt crept over her like a slow, rising fever. She'd ignored the many times he mentioned his health. His comments paved the way for her to ask questions, but instead she chose to ignore them.

"Oh Lord, I treated him horribly last night," she cried aloud. "What am I to do?"

Rick hadn't called. Maybe he had decided to end the relationship.

Bible in hand, Paula ventured outside to the gazebo, where the coolness of morning still blew gently. Again she prayed. As much as she desperately wanted the Lord, it still proved hard to open the Bible. Her stubbornness hung over her like a thundercloud.

With trembling fingers she opened to Joshua 1 and read the instructions God gave His people. When she focused on the passage that Rick had repeated the prior evening, it brought her to her knees. How dear her Lord! Broken and weeping, Paula confessed the sin of faithlessness and a stubborn spirit.

Help me, Father. I want to trust You. I know in my weakness You are my strength, and right now I need direction and faith. Sweet Jesus, thank You for Your everlasting love. Amen.

Paula remembered the quiet solitude of the creek. She yearned to be there with God, and she felt Him beckoning her to come. Clutching the Bible to her heart, she set out for the peacefulness of nature. It took longer than usual to walk the length of the property. She simply lacked any energy. Still the earth alive around her soothed her spirit, and she purposely lingered along the path with an intense desire to see all of God's creation.

Tall grass bent down to form a path through to the fallen tree where she and Rick had sat and talked. It seemed as though the Lord God Himself had prepared a royal carpet into His sanctuary. Seating herself on the same log, Paula opened her Bible and began to read the marked passages that had given her comfort and direction in the past. She didn't know how long she poured over the Scriptures, only that the peace she longed for suddenly took over her spirit. Guidance overcame the past confusion, and Paula could not deny the truth.

She loved Rick Davenport. God had blessed her with him from the moment they first met. How foolish and wrong for her not to accept the gift of love. God never guaranteed life would be painless, but He did promise to be with her all of the way. She had never regretted loving John, and tender memories had replaced the grief of losing him. The thought of living the rest of her life without Rick proved just as painful. John had no choice; God called him home. Losing Rick because of her own stupidity insulted the God who placed them together. If it wasn't too late, she needed to make amends.

Carefully placing her Bible on the log, Paula picked up a stone and tried to skim it across the creek. It plopped and fell without any perfect symmetrical rings of water. Again she sent a stone sailing into the water. This time she twisted her wrist just slightly, but it still fell without effect. She shook her head and smiled. Rick had made it look so easy.

Her eyes drank in a circular flow of water, and she stared at it in disbelief. Challenged by the strange sight, she tried throwing a stone again. Nothing. One more time she saw the flawless ringlets spread out over the creek. Paula smiled and turned around.

"I should have known it was you," she said softly. "How did you know I'd be here?"

"Just a hunch," he said, skimming another stone across the creek. He walked toward her, and Paula felt herself trembling.

"I guess I'll never learn how to make those perfect circles," she managed.

"I could show you," he said, tension drawing them closer.

"I'm pretty stubborn," she replied, taking a step closer. "Rick, I'm so sorry. I've been such a fool."

He gave her a sad smile. "I've done a lot of thinking, and you were right. I should have told you about the heart attack when we first started seeing each other. I admit that I feared your reaction. I'm sorry, too."

Paula held her breath in anticipation. "Can we pick up the pieces?"

"Are you sure?" His eyes searched her face.

They faced each other directly, and Paula hesitated to reach out and touch him.

Paula slowly began. "I don't want to think of my life without you. I love you, Rick, more than I ever thought I could love again. I mean, John and I were young when we married. We grew up together. With you, everything is different, and I don't want to lose another day with you."

Rick grasped her hand firmly in his. "Would you consider growing from middle-age to antique with me?"

Paula's heart raced. "Most definitely." Her eyes glowed. "Do I have to drink green vegetable juice?"

"Oh yes, it would be a part of the prenuptial agreement," he stated with a smile.

"And do I have to walk every morning with you?"

"Absolutely," he replied as a matter-of-fact.

Paula took a deep breath and threw her arms around his neck. "Yes!" she said. "Yes, yes, yes."

He squeezed her tightly before putting her at arm's length. "I have to do this properly," he said solemnly. On the shady bank of the rippling creek, Rick bent to one knee. "Paula Franklin, I love you with all my heart. Will you marry me?"

"Yes," she breathed. "By all that's right and holy, I love you."

Rick reached into his jeans pocket. "When I asked Olivia to marry me, I gave her a diamond ring straight from a fancy jewelry store in Austin." He opened his palm. "This belonged to my grandmother, and I'd like for you to have it."

Paula's eyes swept from his tender gaze to the antique diamond ring in his hand. Never had she seen a piece of jewelry so exquisite, so delicately carved as though the setting had been a fine piece of lace rather than gold.

"Rick, it's beautiful," she breathed, outwardly moved by his gesture of love.

He lifted her left hand and placed it firmly on her finger. "A perfect fit," he whispered. He pulled her close and kissed her gently, then deeply as both shared the beauty of sealed love. And when the moment had passed, they kneeled in the damp moss and thanked God for His gift.

seventeen

"So when is the big day?" Barbara asked excitedly.

Rick and Paula had met Wade and Barbara in Austin for dinner to tell them the news.

Rick grasped Paula's hand firmly. "We've decided to set a date after the hearing; one major event at a time."

"And we want a small wedding," Paula said, "but we do need our favorite couple to assist us."

"In what way?" Wade asked, glancing up from his menu.

Rick turned to Paula. "Do you want to ask them or shall I?"

"I don't know, Rick," Paula said with a tone of indecision. "We don't have to ask them right now, maybe another time."

"Okay you two," Wade laughed. "Out with it or there won't be a moment of peace until you do."

"And I'll go crazy," Barbara added with a toss of her blond head.

"Um," Paula said thoughtfully, suppressing a laugh. "I need a matron of honor."

"And I need a best man," Rick interjected. "Do you two have any candidates?"

He broke into a hearty laugh, a deep contagious laugh.

As the waiter approached the table, Wade and Barbara instantly accepted the offer. Once they gave their food order, Barbara became a host of questions.

"Slow down," Paula laughed. She squeezed a slice of lemon into her water and purposely hesitated to answer her friend.

"I hate it when you make me wait," Barbara said, feigning impatience.

"I know," Paula breathed. "But it is much more fun watching you squirm. Now, in reply to your first question, Rick and I plan to marry and live at The Country Charm."

"After all, that is where we met," he pointed out.

Barbara looked at Rick curiously. "What about your beautiful home?"

"Um, I don't know yet. I've thought of offering it to one of the kids, but if they aren't interested, I'll put it on the market."

"Who is going to perform the ceremony?" Wade asked.

Rick grinned broadly. "We haven't talked to a minister yet, but we really like the young man who pastors our church in Brenham. And Irene has begged us to cater the wedding, including baking the cake. She wants to cook a huge dinner for all the guests, and with the way she cooks, how could we refuse?"

"So will it be inside or outside of The Country Charm?" Barbara asked excitedly.

Paula glanced at Rick and he kissed her nose before she gave Barbara her attention. "I think it will be a simple ceremony, possibly outside in the gazebo." She turned to Rick. "Did I leave anything out?"

"A honeymoon?" Wade asked curiously.

"Of course," Rick replied. "We'll probably take a few days and go somewhere, but I'd like to take Paula to Hawaii when the tourist season slackens a bit."

"How romantic," Barbara crooned. "But I knew you two were meant for each other the first time I saw you bending over a set of blueprints. Something clicked, even if I was the only one who saw it."

"Oh, we had a feeling," Rick assured her, "except Paula and I were too busy with the renovation project."

The merriment continued from the appetizers to the last sip of coffee.

"An autumn wedding means the temperatures ought to be a little cooler," Wade pointed out as they all stepped out into the humid night air.

"Right," Rick agreed. "Of course, if I had my way we'd marry the day after the hearing, but I guess my lady needs a day or two to get ready."

The four drove back to Wade and Barbara's house and

talked way into the night, and not once did anyone mention Kristi. Paula had not felt this happy in many years. She didn't mind the giddy schoolgirl emotions or the way she continually found Rick's eyes locked onto hers. This was love, pure and simple, and she adored every minute of it. The precious part of the whole evening centered on sharing their wedding plans with dear friends.

A wave of sadness swept over Paula. If only she could share her joy with Kristi. She didn't dare contact her daughter; James had told her specifically not to initiate any type of communication. *I will not let this ruin my wonderful evening,* she told herself fiercely. *Tonight is a celebration of God's plan for our lives. I trust in Him to supply all my needs, and that includes bringing Kristi back to Him.*

As the truck sped along the highway toward Brenham, Rick and Paula talked about their future together. His children had expressed their love and support for the upcoming marriage and eagerly welcomed her into the family. In many ways, Paula wished the wedding could be sooner. Now that they had confessed their love, she wanted to exchange the marriage vows. Only the hearing stood in their way, and she refused to think of any outcome other than the judge dismissing the case.

る

The next four weeks kept Paula busy between The Country Charm and spending every spare moment with Rick. Now that they knew they were to be married, their time together became more precious. Those around them teased and pointed out the stars in their eyes and their preoccupation with each other, but the couple didn't mind. Everything about their love seemed perfect.

The outcome of the hearing still plagued Paula. She'd given the matter over to God time and time again only to allow the nagging doubts and concerns to overtake her once more. *Worrying is a sin and a lack of trust in God,* she thought, except a part of her feared the outcome. How humiliating if she were forced to undergo psychiatric evaluation. *God will be with me if that happens,* she thought. *I can be strong and courageous.*

❧

The morning of the hearing held little promise as lightning seared across the sky and thunder roared angrily. Rick had joined her early for breakfast, but neither had an appetite.

"I hope this is not an indication of the day," Paula said, noting the dismal weather. She picked up her purse along with an umbrella. "Can we pray before we drive into Austin?"

Rick hugged her tightly, and she felt a surge of tears threatening to spill over her cheeks. Quickly she whisked them away as Rick prayed for God's will to be done and the happenings in court to glorify Him.

"I apologize for being so quiet," she said as the truck braved the driving rain. "It's hard to be optimistic with this storm."

Rick reached across the seat and gathered her hand into his. "It will soon be over, honey, and we can get on with our lives."

"But what if the judge orders a psychiatric evaluation?" Paula whispered, staring out the window.

"Then we will handle it, but I truly have a peace about today. Remember your lawyer is a good Christian who has been praying just like we have. He has the case prepared for your defense, and there is no indication of a problem."

Paula nodded. "I know; I just want it to be over. It all goes back to the fact that my own daughter is against me. I'm so hurt and confused about Kristi's actions."

"Of course you are," he said gently. "Why don't you look in the console for my Bible and read aloud to me. I think Scripture will take your mind off this whole thing."

Paula turned and smiled into his crystal blue eyes. Of course he was right. She needed to focus on God, not on herself. They had talked before about what would happen if the case went to trial. Rick wanted to give in to Kristi's demands and take care of Paula himself, but she didn't feel the same way. Her daughter's accusations were wrong, and Paula intended to fight the lawsuit every inch of the way.

As they traveled closer to Austin, the thunder and lightning passed, but the heavy rain continued. Rick drove into a parking lot beside the Texas State Civil Court building and the two dodged the weather under the shelter of umbrellas.

"I forgot to thank you for all you've done," Paula said once inside. "And you look very handsome this morning."

"You're welcome, and as I stated earlier, you look awesome in that green suit."

Paula couldn't help but laugh. "Where did you get the word 'awesome'?"

"Oh, from grandkids, where else?"

He had succeeded in calming her nerves, and a squeeze of his hand reminded her of the supreme Judge who would be right with her.

Rick spotted Kristi standing alone near the courtroom entrance. When he pointed her out, Paula saw a stranger before her. Kristi looked as though she'd aged. Lines creased across her brow, and her face appeared devoid of color. Paula's heart went out to her; she wanted desperately to take her daughter into her arms and hold her. Only then did she realize the inner turmoil of an angry young woman without God. All of this time Paula had been thinking more about what Kristi attempted to do rather than her daughter's emotional state, and she felt ashamed of her selfishness. Granted, Paula had prayed for Kristi's return to the Lord, but not for Him to calm His wayward child. She caught Kristi's eyes and smiled warmly, but the young woman looked away, clearly annoyed.

Heavenly Father, Kristi is so miserable, Paula prayed. *I'm sorry for not praying specifically for her well-being. She needs You, Lord. Soften her heart and bring her to reconciliation with You. I don't care about the outcome of today, only that my beloved child finds peace again. In Jesus' holy name, Amen.*

James Sharp emerged from the elevator and greeted Paula and Rick. "Don't worry about a thing," he said. "I firmly believe the judge will throw this out as soon as we present our case."

"Do you have any idea what Kristi's attorney is basing his argument on?" Rick asked.

James shook his head. "I called him, but he refused to comment. Let's go on inside and go over a few things."

Rick placed his hand on the small of Paula's back and supported her past Kristi and a young gentleman. Paula assumed he was her lawyer.

At the appointed time, the bailiff called "All rise" to those seated in the courtroom. Paula allowed Rick to steady her. She felt physically weak, but not nauseous. She felt frightened, but she had a sense of peace. Giving Rick a shaky smile, she turned her attention to the judge.

As suspected, Kristi's attorney based Paula's incompetence upon a series of financial decisions made since John Franklin's death.

"Mrs. Franklin did not have sound legal and financial advice before proceeding with the purchase of the property in Brenham," Kristi's attorney stated. "A local contractor, by the name of Rick Davenport, bid extremely low on the project. My client fears he purposely secured the bid in order to win Mrs. Franklin's affections. My client saw firsthand Mr. Davenport's ability to charm his way into Mrs. Franklin's life. It has become evident to my client that Mr. Davenport seeks to obtain control of Mrs. Franklin's money. At my client's request, a private detective watched Mrs. Franklin's home. Mr. Davenport makes daily stops at the bed-and-breakfast, and the two are often seen together in public.

"My client is a successful stock broker, and she is only interested in her mother's welfare and in protecting her financial assets. Miss Franklin claims her mother has experienced severe mental problems since her husband's death five years ago. She has become the target of numerous charities and has contributed an exorbitant amount of money to her church. The state of Mrs. Franklin's affairs has caused considerable anguish for her daughter. In short, Paula Franklin needs someone to manage her financial affairs before the funds are depleted."

Kristi's lawyer concluded his petition and presented the judge with the detective's report on Rick and various forms of which Paula had no idea of the content.

James rose to address the judge. Paula felt her heart pound against her chest. She detested having to prove her credibility; more so, she despised the questioning of Rick's character.

The calm, professional voice of James Sharp instantly put Paula at ease. How could she have doubted a Christian lawyer who prayed over his clients?

"Your Honor, I have for your examination several documents that will prove beyond a shadow of a doubt that Paula Franklin is indeed of sound mind. She has exercised wisdom and discretion in her personal and financial decisions since the death of John Franklin some five years ago.

"The first document is a financial statement. It proves her investments have been made wisely with the counsel of a financial planner and an accountant.

"The second document is a detailed statement of Mrs. Franklin's recently acquired business, The Country Charm. It shows the price she paid for the property, well below the appraised value, and the separate bids for the renovation project. Please note the piece of property originally belonged to Mr. Davenport's grandmother, which is why he bid lower than the other contractors. Mr. Davenport has a personal and sentimental interest in the success of Mrs. Franklin's bed-and-breakfast.

"The final document for the court's inspection is Mr. Davenport's personal financial statement. Attached are four letters of recommendation from various professionals from the Brenham area. If it pleases the court, note Mr. Davenport is quite wealthy in his own right, far more than Mrs. Franklin.

"Your Honor, what we have here is a case of a young woman who desires control of her mother's finances for personal gain. There is nothing in Mrs. Franklin's life to indicate that she is mentally incompetent or unfit to carry out business and financial matters."

James returned to his chair, and the judge examined all the documents presented to him.

"Thank you, James," she whispered. "You were wonderful."

He patted her hand lightly. "I believe in your competence, and God will honor your prayers."

Paula waited breathlessly. She turned around to where Rick sat, and they exchanged smiles. He looked as confident as she felt. It pleased her to see Wade and Barbara seated next to him, and she nodded in their direction. Barbara mouthed, "We love you," and the gesture made Paula smile.

The judge cleared his throat, gaining everyone's attention. "I see no purpose in wasting the court's time any further in this matter. This case shouldn't have gotten this far. It is a waste of attorney fees and taxpayers' money. Young lady," his eyebrows raised to meet Kristi's gaze, "I'm not sure what you were trying to accomplish with a suit against your mother, but I see Mrs. Franklin as a competent, intelligent woman who had the guts to start her own business. She's done a thorough job, and from the financial status I see before me, her bed-and-breakfast is off to an excellent start. Case dismissed."

"Thank You, Lord," Paula breathed. She hugged James and thanked him for representing her. Instantly Rick stood at her side; his face glowed from the good news. Behind him, Wade and Barbara greeted her with warm congratulations.

"Sweetheart, it's over," she said to Rick. "We can go on with our lives now."

As Rick hugged her again, she peered over his shoulder and saw Kristi. The sight of her daughter ceased any further thought of celebration. Kristi couldn't control her composure; rage seethed from her face. She obviously blamed her attorney for losing the case, and her fury unleashed upon him.

Paula stiffened and Rick released his hold on her. He searched her face anxiously.

"It's Kristi," she explained. "She looks more angry than ever."

Rick, too, glanced in the direction of the opposing attorney and his client. "I agree, and I had hoped settling this mess would bring you two back together."

Paula sighed. "I'm going to try to talk to her."

Rick gave her an encouraging smile, and she slowly walked across the courtroom to her daughter. As Paula approached, Kristi stopped berating her attorney and glared at her mother.

"Kristi, I'm sorry about all of the ugliness between us. Can we put it all behind us and move on?" Paula asked sincerely.

Indignation etched across Kristi's face. "How can you

even suggest such a thing? You've ruined my future and embarrassed me here today. It's your fault I'm out attorney and court fees, Mother. If you would have agreed to let me manage your finances, this could have been avoided. But, oh no, you had to make me look like a fool."

Paula felt pity and astonishment at the same time. "How can you accuse me of such things? This was your own doing, Kristi. You forced me to seek legal counsel to protect myself, and I did. You lost the suit because you were wrong." She swallowed hard to keep from losing her temper.

"Whatever, Mother. You just go on back to your sweet little bed-and-breakfast and your country bumpkin boyfriend; I have no further use for you."

Paula bit her lip to keep from saying more. She let out a deep breath and joined her friends rather than create an unpleasant scene.

"We heard," Rick said softly. "Honey, I'm sorry."

"Me, too," she said. Seeing her beloved friends reminded her of what Kristi had lost in her senseless rebellion. "Kristi's bitterness is really sad."

"Unfortunately yes," Wade said. "She's definitely not the same girl I remember."

Paula turned to both of her friends. "God will draw her back to Him; I'm sure of it."

In the lobby of the court building, good-byes were said to Barbara, Wade, and James. Outside the rain beat down in an unrelenting downpour. The dark sky seemed to darken Paula's mood, sending her into a well of depression.

"Are you going to be sick?" Rick asked once they were inside the truck.

She shook her head. "No, and I'm not going to cry, either. God brought us through a victorious battle today, and I'm going to pull myself up to praise Him for his righteous judgment."

"That's my girl," Rick encouraged.

"But Kristi's welfare still makes me sad," she added, pulling his Bible from the console. "Can I read to you again?"

Rick nodded with a smile.

eighteen

When the two returned, Irene had filled the house with the aroma of coffee and the sweet, spicy smells of fresh baked apple pies. She greeted Rick and Paula at the door with a hug and a sincere smile. Paula appreciated Irene so much, and the touch of her friend nearly brought the tears she'd sworn not to cry. Rick relayed the judge's decision.

"Praise God it's over," Irene said. "But it is still an unhappy day when a daughter sues her mother."

Paula agreed. "Thank you for being here today. When we opened the door and I could smell your wonderful cooking, I knew I was home."

"You are very welcome," Irene said simply. "I didn't want you returning to an empty house. And of course I had to bake something. Oh, Paula, you look so tired. Why don't you rest? Everything is done for tonight's guests."

Paula felt exhausted. "That sounds like a wonderful idea. Do you mind?" Paula asked Rick.

"Honey, I have things to do, so I'll catch up with you later," he replied.

She walked him to the door. So many thoughts raced through her mind, but she desperately needed rest. Hazel eyes met crystal blue.

"Honey, I want to hug you and curl up next to you, but I'm so tired I can't think," she confessed.

"We'll talk later; maybe we could plan something for Sunday afternoon."

Soon afterward Paula crawled into bed, feeling every bit like a child who had played too hard all day, except she wasn't a child and the day hadn't been fun. The last thought written across her mind came in the form of a prayer for Kristi.

❧

Sunday afternoon found Rick and Paula off for a few hours alone. "I want to set a date for the wedding," Paula said as the two strolled hand in hand along one of the paths of a nearby rose garden. The eight acres hosted a huge array of various antique roses, a wildflower and herb meadow, and garden favorites arranged around restored buildings of another era. She stopped to smell a pink rose. "Rick, am I being too assertive?"

He chuckled. "Don't think so; I wanted to get married yesterday."

"It's just seeing these flowers reminds me of a wedding."

"You say when, I'll be there," Rick hastily replied.

Paula playfully poked at his ribs. "Any preference of time?"

Rick pretended that she'd injured him. "No. My only requirement is that you will be there with the pastor."

"I agree." Paula fought the urge to throw her arms around his neck. "But when?"

He thought for a minute. "I realize we need to work around the bed-and-breakfast and guest reservations. What about mid-September? Can we put together a small wedding by then?"

Paula smiled. "Yes, sir, we can. Irene still wants to cater a dinner; in fact, she is all set. I don't think any of the preparations should be difficult."

Rick planted a quick kiss on her cheek, and they continued their tour through the sweet scent of flowers. She smiled happily to herself. Being Rick's wife meant more to her than a whole field of roses.

By the time the two enjoyed dinner and attended church, darkness had settled.

She snuggled next to Rick all the way home, reveling in their afternoon together. Fortunately, there were no guests that evening. When they reached the rambling farmhouse, Paula's answering machine flashed with eight new messages.

"Back to reality," Paula laughed as she pressed the play button. The first five messages involved reservations and inquiries for information about The Country Charm. Message six caught her totally unaware.

"Mrs. Paula Franklin, this is St. David's Hospital in Austin. Your daughter, Kristi, has been involved in a car accident, and we would like for you to call us right away. She needs a blood transfusion as soon as possible. Please call the hospital at 512-476-7111 and ask for emergency. Thank you."

Silence permeated the room. Both Rick and Paula were stunned by the sudden news. Rick rewound the tape, pressed the play button again, and increased the volume. This time he jotted down the hospital's number. He glanced into Paula's pale face.

"Here, I'll dial the number and you talk to the hospital," he said with one arm firmly supporting her waist.

She nodded and lifted the receiver to her ear. All the while her heart drummed furiously against her chest. "Yes, may I have emergency, please?" She wrapped her hand around Rick's fingers. "This is Paula Franklin. I received a message about my daughter's car accident. . ."

Moments later, Paula replaced the phone. "Kristi needs blood right away, and we have the same rare type." She swallowed hard. "The nurse said that Kristi's in critical condition."

Rick picked up her purse and dropped the house keys inside it. "Let's go. We'll pray on the way to Austin."

"It's the hospital on 32nd Street, just off I-35," Paula said, as though in a daze. She followed Rick to the truck, all the while praying for Kristi's life.

As soon as they were on the road, Rick phoned Wade with the news. Their friends planned to leave immediately for the hospital.

"I'm so scared that I can't pray," Paula admitted. "All I can think is Jesus, Jesus, help my little girl."

"Honey, you've said it all when you call upon the name of Jesus. He knows your heart and what Kristi needs."

She felt her stomach begin to churn. "Oh, Rick, my faith seems so weak right now."

"Let Jesus be your strength," he urged.

She rubbed her hands together; they were cold and clammy.

Even her feet felt numb, and the outside temperature registered ninety degrees. As though sensing her discomfort, Rick switched off the air-conditioner.

"Would you call the hospital and see if there's been any change?" she asked.

Rick's phone call to St. David's revealed nothing new. Flashes of Kristi's life swept across Paula's mind. She remembered the first time the doctor laid the newborn in her arms. One look at her infant daughter brought an overwhelming love and a sense of protection unlike anything she'd ever experienced. As vivid as today was the toddler who mirrored her daddy and loved to have him play with her. Paula recalled the first day of kindergarten and how she and John both cried when the teacher said they had to say good-bye at the door. Paula saw the scenes of yesterday in Kristi's first ballet recital when she wore Heidi braids and danced every step. The years of cheerleading, driving lessons, and Kristi's excitement over her first car played across Paula's mind like an open scrapbook. Her precious daughter's life held such promise, and her future looked wonderful until John's unexpected death. Paula closed her eyes and imagined Kristi holding onto the hand of God and clutching His fingers for life.

Rick broke every speed limit in Texas while driving to Austin. At one point Paula feared they wouldn't get to the hospital in one piece, but she didn't want him to slow down. Nothing mattered but getting to Kristi. Traffic lights blinked green in their favor, and soon the two pulled into the emergency parking area of St. David's Hospital.

As if in a daze and merely going through the motions of life, Paula instinctively latched onto Rick's hand as they rushed through the emergency doors. At the information desk, she introduced herself and explained the circumstances. Instantly a nurse appeared and escorted them into an elevator and up to intensive care. The nurse suggested they wait in the small waiting room outside the care unit while she contacted the doctor.

Paula heard voices and whirled around to see Barbara and Wade seated in the small room. "You are so good for coming.

Has anyone told you anything?"

Barbara rushed to her side. "No, nothing. We hoped you two had word."

The nurse interrupted any more conversation. "As you know, we need blood right away. I realize all of this must be a shock to you, but we don't have much time."

"Can't I see her first?" Paula's voice rang near hysteria.

"They are preparing her for surgery," the nurse said kindly, yet firmly. She looked into Paula's face. "I'll see what I can do; follow me."

"Can my fiancé come with me?" Paula asked, keeping step with the nurse.

"I'm sorry, but only immediate family. He can wait for you in the waiting room."

Paula looked back at Rick. He stood with his hands in his pockets, looking every bit as helpless as she felt.

"I'll be praying," he stated firmly.

Nothing prepared Paula for the physical condition of her daughter. Kristi's face was swollen beyond recognition and ugly bruises dominated most of her lovely features. Paula instantly recognized a heart monitor, and she fought the rising panic threatening to overcome her. One nurse checked her pulse; another adjusted the flow of an IV. Two doctors barked directions and another nurse scurried about.

"Mrs. Franklin," one of the doctors called, without taking his eyes from a chart before him. "We need to get your daughter into surgery, and I understand you are willing to donate blood." His words sounded cold and formal.

"Yes, sir. Can you tell me about Kristi's injuries?"

The doctor lifted his eyes long enough to nod affirmatively. "A surgical procedure is required to stop internal bleeding. That is our gravest concern. The impact of the accident knocked her unconscious, but the X rays do not indicate anything more than a concussion. Her right femur is broken in several places and will require surgery after we have stabilized her." He took a quick breath and checked the heart monitor. "We strongly suspect both arms are fractured, most likely due to gripping the steering wheel upon impact. That is all we have at this time. Mrs. Franklin, we need to get your daughter into surgery."

The doctor's urgency pushed Paula back into reality. She thanked him as they rolled Kristi's bed out of the room.

"He is one of the best doctors on staff," the nurse said as though reading her mind.

"I forgot to ask him if he was Christian," Paula said, wringing her hands.

The nurse took both of Paula's clammy hands. "He's not, but his assistant is a born-again believer."

Paula's eyes flew to the nurse's face. "And you are, too?"

"Yes, and as soon as we draw your blood, we'll pray together."

A myriad of questions floated through Paula's mind as the nurse drew the unit of blood. Rick sat beside her quietly, like a gentle giant, while the nurse attempted to answer her rambling of questions.

"How bad do you think she is?" Paula asked softly, staring into the nurse's face, looking for a facial expression to calm her frenzied nerves.

"I don't know any more than you," she said. "But I do believe in the power of prayer, and our God is a God of healing."

nineteen

Paula detested the sterile, septic smell of hospitals. It reminded her of incurable diseases and the threat of death. Pastel uniforms and white shoes marched silently past the intensive care waiting room, appearing and disappearing like passing ghosts. Little sound met her ears except for the closing of an airtight door or the creaking of life-sustaining equipment down the hall. The deafening rumble of time beat against her temples as minutes ticked by like hours. And still the doctors hovered over Kristi's nearly lifeless form.

"Why don't you two go on home," Paula finally suggested to Wade and Barbara. "It's no telling how long before we get word."

"I agree," Rick said. "You two need to get some sleep. Wade, you've got to go to work in the morning. There's no sense in both of you wearing yourselves out."

Wade shook his head. "I believe we need to be here when Kristi comes out of surgery." He glanced at his wife.

Barbara agreed. "We want to be here until the surgery is over."

"Thank you," Rick said, running his fingers through his hair. "Could we pray together again? I'm a firm believer in pestering God."

Paula wanted to pray audibly, but her thoughts jumbled from one concern about Kristi to another, so she allowed her dear friends to say the words she couldn't. And the time inched slowly by, hour after hour with no word from the doctor.

Shortly after seven the next morning, a doctor entered the waiting room.

Visibly exhausted, he sat in a chair before addressing them.

"Mrs. Franklin, I assisted with your daughter's surgery. She is now in intensive care rather than recovery. We successfully stopped the internal bleeding, but she is in critical condition. Twice we thought we had lost her, but miraculously she pulled through. The next twenty-four hours are the most crucial. If we are able to stabilize her, then we can go back in to repair her leg." He paused. "The nurse told me that you are a Christian, which is why I wanted to visit with you myself. She needs prayer not only for her physical body. For some reason she is not fighting like we would expect. I'm telling you this so you can pray specifically, just as I have been."

Paula felt the tears flow unchecked. She buried her face in her hands while Rick wrapped his arm around her.

"Thank you, doctor," Rick said, "for your healing prayers and visiting with us."

Paula lifted her head and with a tear-stained face she attempted a brave smile. "May God bless you, and I thank Him for sending you to us."

"You're welcome, Mrs. Franklin. Shall we all pray for your daughter?"

A few moments later, the doctor rose to leave. He planned to stay at the hospital for a few more hours until Kristi's condition improved.

"When can Paula see her daughter?" Rick asked.

"Possibly soon. I'll send a nurse to let you know." He left them, and the four were once more alone.

Wade took a deep breath. "It sure would be nice if more doctors were Christian. That man cares about his patients and their families."

"True," Paula said. "His prayer for her spirit really touched me. Now I want to pray over her and beg her to fight this thing."

"I've read accountings of people hearing what was being said while under anesthetic," Barbara said gently.

Rick cleared his throat and hesitated. "My guess is she doesn't think anyone loves her. It's hard to fight for life when there's nothing worth fighting for."

"Honey, I want you with me when I see her," Paula whispered. "She needs to know we both love her."

He nodded in agreement, and they sat down to wait again.

Within a half-hour, Rick and Paula were allowed a few moments with Kristi. She hadn't regained consciousness, but Paula felt a deep urgency to be at her side. She touched her daughter's face. Kristi's normally pink cheeks and vibrant skin had been replaced with an ashen paleness.

"You're going to make it through this," she whispered. "But you have to fight. I love you, my precious baby. If you can hear anything at all, please know I love you, and I want you to live. So many people are praying for you." Paula caught herself sobbing. She wanted to be strong and sure of Kristi's recovery, not captured in tears. "We can mend the differences separating us. Things between us can be good; I'm sure of it. Just fight for life, honey. The Lord will help you."

Rick stood on the opposite side of the bed. When he reached across Kristi to grasp both of Paula's hands, she saw tears in his eyes, too.

"Rick, pray for me. All I'm doing is sobbing and rambling."

"Oh God, our Father, the great Healer," he began, "we come to You on Kristi's behalf. She's so young with so much of life ahead of her. We ask for grace and mercy through Your healing power and to give her the will to live. We have no idea of the pain that she is in, but You do. Only You can comfort and deliver her. Give her mother and I a chance to show her how much we love her. Oh Lord, I looked forward to this baby girl in my life. If this is a selfish prayer, then I beg forgiveness, but I pray for healing and life. In Your Son Jesus' holy and perfect name, Amen."

Again Paula and Rick confined themselves to the intensive care area. They tried to eat, but food didn't settle well with either of them. Paula phoned Irene at home and explained what had happened. Her dear friend told her not to worry about the bed-and-breakfast; she'd handle affairs until Paula could return. Rick talked to Lupe and discussed what business needed to be done.

After Wade and Barbara went home to shower, Barbara offered to drive to Brenham for Rick and Paula's clothes and toiletries. Her suggestion came as an answer to prayer, for neither wanted to leave the hospital for any length of time.

Early in the afternoon, Kristi woke briefly. She moaned in pain and a nurse quickly administered medication that put her back to sleep. The bedside vigil continued. A few hours later, the doctor who performed the surgery announced, much to his surprise, that Kristi had taken definite steps toward healing.

"She had no will to live," he said incredulously. "I don't know what happened, except she is slowly gaining strength."

"We do," Paula said. "God has heard our prayers."

The doctor shrugged his shoulders. He apparently didn't believe in a supreme God. He probably thought Kristi's improvement was merely a twist of chance. As long as her vital signs improved, they could schedule the surgery for her leg.

Paula phoned Barbara as her friend drove to Brenham. "Kristi's second surgery is scheduled for sometime Wednesday or Thursday. Once her leg is repaired, then I will feel more comfortable in asking questions about her recovery."

"So has she been removed from the critical list?" Barbara asked.

"Yes, praise God. She's now termed as stable, and I truly believe she's out of real danger."

Later that evening, Rick persuaded Paula to rest a few hours at Wade and Barbara's. He insisted she get some rest.

"I'll wait here," Rick said. "I'll call if anything changes."

Paula consented to a shower, but she returned to the hospital within an hour for Rick to shower and change, too. Both refused to spend the night anywhere except in Kristi's room. Exhausted, yet committed, the couple slept restlessly in the visitor chairs, taking turns watching over Kristi.

On Wednesday afternoon, after the second surgery, Kristi aroused long enough to recognize her mother and Rick.

"Mother," Kristi whispered through parched lips.

Instantly Paula hovered over the bed. "Yes, honey, I'm right here."

"What happened?" Kristi closed her eyes and wet her lips.

"You were involved in a car accident," Paula said gently.

"Would you like a little ice on your lips?"

"Yes, please. My mouth is so dry. When did you come?"

"Sunday night the hospital called me, and Rick and I came right on."

She opened her eyes and studied Rick standing beside her mother. She said nothing for several moments. "I remember now. My car went out of control, and I. . .I don't know what happened then."

"Are you in much pain?" Paula asked.

"Yes," Kristi replied as perspiration beaded on her forehead. "What happened to me? I hurt all over."

"You've had two surgeries, honey, one to stop internal bleeding and another to mend your right leg. But you are going to be just fine. Why don't you rest, and we can talk later."

Kristi closed her eyes. "So is this Monday?"

"No, this is Wednesday," Paula said softly with a sigh.

"Three days gone," Kristi whispered.

"Just go back to sleep," Paula urged. "Rest will help you the most."

Kristi's eyes opened again. "Have you been here all this time?"

"Yes, we have," Paula replied. "Except for an occasional run to the cafeteria or a trip to Wade and Barbara's to shower."

Tears filled Kristi's eyes and rolled down her cheeks. "After all I've done?" And she drifted back to sleep.

Two hours later she woke when a nurse checked her pulse. "You've come a long way, little lady," the plump nurse declared. "My, but don't you have beautiful eyes."

Kristi attempted a faint smile. "I have my father's eyes."

The nurse glanced at Rick. "I'm not her father," he said. "He passed away five years ago."

"I could have answered her," Kristi said irritably.

"Yes, I guess you could," Rick responded, and a line deepened across his brow.

Paula's spirits took a nosedive. She'd hoped Kristi would have mellowed about her feelings toward Rick, but obviously not. A surge of anger raced through Paula's veins. *Rick has been at her side during this whole ordeal! Why can't she see his devotion?* As though reading her thoughts, Rick smiled encouragingly. Their eyes met, and understanding poured from his face.

"You two can leave now," Kristi announced. "I don't need a babysitter."

The nurse hurriedly finished the testing and left the room.

"Granted you don't need a babysitter," Rick said, standing and walking to her bedside. "But your mother needs to make sure you are going to be all right."

"Don't I have a doctor?" Kristi snapped, avoiding his face.

Paula stood and joined Rick. "We want to be here with you."

"Mother, you haven't been here for me in years. Go on home to your little cottage in the country. I don't want you in this room, and I don't want you in my life."

Paula pressed her lips together and trembled slightly. "I'm sorry you feel this way, but unfortunately I can't do that. You see, you aren't able to take care of yourself, and as soon as the doctor releases you, well, you're coming to Brenham with me."

"Over my dead body," Kristi seethed and clutched the sides of her bed rail.

"Dear, you almost got your wish with that remark, but never mind." Paula patted her daughter just above where the cast encased her arm. "You have no choice in the matter. It's already arranged."

"I can take care of myself."

Paula smiled sadly. "I wish you could, honey. Once you're a little more awake you will find a badly fractured leg, both of your arms in casts, your ribs are broken, and of course there's still a good amount of healing needed to be done internally. I don't want to bother you with all of the things you can't do right now, but I'm sure you will recognize them soon enough."

"Why, I'll hire a nurse," Kristi spurted.

"Sorry, it's all been taken care of." Paula gave Rick her attention. "I'm ready for a good meal, how about you?"

twenty

Two weeks later, Paula brought Kristi to The Country Charm. If she appreciated the change in the hundred-year-old farmhouse, she didn't say, for Kristi had refused to speak since leaving the hospital. Paula chose to ignore her stubborn daughter and chatted away about matters at the bed-and-breakfast.

When Paula pulled into her driveway, she spotted Rick's truck and saw him near the barn talking to Keifer. Irene met her in the driveway with Harry yapping at her heels. It felt good to be home.

Paula hugged Irene closely, then bent to pat the collie puppy. "Oh, my little Harry. I've missed you, and goodness how you've grown."

"He hasn't had an accident in three days," Irene said proudly. She peeked in the back seat and smiled broadly. "I'm Irene; welcome to The Country Charm."

Kristi turned her head and stared out the opposite window. Paula silently apologized for her daughter's rudeness.

"Well, shall we help you inside?" Paula asked cheerfully. "Rick has built a ramp for your wheelchair at the back entrance." She saw him walking their way and wondered what would transpire while he helped Kristi from the truck. At least her daughter might now have something to say.

"Hi honey," he greeted and planted a kiss on Paula's forehead. "And how is Kristi doing?" He smiled at Kristi, but she said nothing. The young woman continued her blank stare, avoiding any type of eye contact. With a confident look, Rick lifted the wheelchair from the back of Paula's sport utility vehicle and pushed it along the passenger side. He opened the door and leaned on it briefly. "It's been a long time since I carried a pretty lady, but I'm ready if you are."

Kristi's fuming glare left no need for words. Gingerly he lifted her from the seat, paying close attention to both broken arms and the leg sealed in a cast from her upper thigh to her foot. Paula steadied the wheelchair while he gently set Kristi down. She said nothing as Rick began pushing her toward the house.

Paula smiled, hoping he saw her gratitude. "Is everything all right with Keifer?" she asked.

"Yes, he wanted me to see the newly painted carriage. It looks great. When Kristi is feeling better, she'll have to see all the different sights here."

Irene laughed. "Just seeing what you two have done to the house is a wonderful experience."

"Kristi hasn't been here since I bought it," Paula informed her.

"Oh my, then she's in for a treat," Irene replied.

As Rick pushed Kristi toward the back porch, Paula studied her daughter's face for a reaction to the new surroundings. The high grass that Kristi had feared contained snakes had been replaced with landscaping, a flower garden, and a gazebo. A spark of interest caused the young woman to lift her chin, but she remained silent. Once inside, Kristi seemed disinterested and bored.

"When you are ready, I'll take you on a tour of the house," Paula said. "I'm putting you in a room downstairs. It's right beside mine but has its own bath. Oddly enough, I decorated it in the colors of your room back in Austin, pink and a touch of spruce green. I hope you like it."

Kristi's eyes flew wide when Rick wheeled her into the designated bedroom.

"The bed is an heirloom from your father's family. I had it in storage for many years simply because I had no place to put it." Paula walked across the hardwood floor and traced the carving on the walnut headboard. "This headboard always reminds me of a queen's throne. The lace and spindles are so elegant, yet feminine. I haven't put any guests in here yet; I guess I had you in mind."

Kristi slowly studied every inch of the room from the pale pink walls, the pink rose and spruce green window treatment, an area rug in the same colors, and the white eyelet bedspread, ruffle, and pillows. Swedish ivy draped from a plant stand in front of a window while dried rose swags and silk rose arrangements graced the room. Her eyes set upon a marble-topped English washstand, and Paula thought she saw a faint smile.

"The small green armoire with the distressed finish was an easy find, but I did stencil the pink roses myself. Do you remember the Victorian lounging sofa from your grandmother's parlor? Well, luckily I found a marble-topped table in the same cherry wood to go with it. The nightstand came from Grandmother's things, too." Paula paused and placed her forefinger upon her lips. "Goodness, let me see. The closet is not too large, so let me know if you need more space. Oh, my, I hope you like the bathroom. I felt rather creative or maybe impetuous when I decorated it. The pink and green wallpaper is basic enough, but I had the claw-foot bathtub painted green and stenciled in the same pattern as the armoire. There's lots of storage, and the cabinetry is empty." Paula glanced at Kristi's face. "Oh, I'm sorry; I'm rambling."

"You really enjoyed doing all of this," Kristi stated with seemingly no emotion.

"Yes, very much," Paula replied simply. "Someday, if you want, I'll show you the scrapbook your father and I started when you were still in grade school. This has been many years in the making. It's been a blessing to see it become a reality."

Silence permeated the room.

"I'll go get her things from the truck," Rick announced. "Just bring them in here?"

"Yes, Rick, that'll be fine."

Once Kristi saw he had left the room, she turned the wheelchair around to see the bathroom. "How much of this house did he do?"

"From beginning to the end he helped right along beside me."

"Are you two getting married?" Kristi's question sounded cold and flat.

Paula felt a little taken back by the question. "Ah. . .yes, we are. The wedding is in three weeks. We plan to be married here."

"I see," Kristi said, wetting her lips.

To break the dreadful silence gathering around them, Paula asked if the room suited her.

"I guess if I have to stay here, this room will do."

Paula masked the well of depression building inside of her. Maybe bringing Kristi here wasn't God's will. What if she had made a terrible mistake? In her effort to be a mother to Kristi, she may have ignored God's guidance. And Rick. . .she already feared Kristi's attitude may affect their relationship. For that matter, how could she endure the sarcasm and caustic tongue?

Pride had a great deal to do with Paula's feelings. She'd literally poured herself into the old house, and to hear the room would merely "do" not only hurt her feelings, but made her a bit angry. *God is still in control,* she told herself. *And it's a good thing, because I'd still like to turn her across my knee.*

❧

A few days later, Paula basked in the late afternoon shade with the lazy sounds of summer calling her weary body to peace. She snuggled against Rick's shoulder and closed her eyes, allowing the rhythm of the glider to calm her weary body. For a few precious moments she forgot Kristi's bitter words over the past three days. Mother-daughter time had not been at all what she had envisioned—far from it.

Rick played with a strand of Paula's hair, and his fingers against her cheeks caused her to sigh dreamily. "What are you thinking?" he asked softly.

"Us," she said smiling. "Two and a half weeks and we will be Mr. and Mrs. Rick Davenport."

"Um," he said dreamily. "Seems like an eternity."

"Especially with my charming houseguest," she added.

"Honey, Kristi will come around. She just needs time."

Paula felt her own body grow tense. "But how are we supposed to start a new life together with Kristi's continual complaining? She hasn't been anywhere except her room and the kitchen. Oh, I'm sorry for whining. It's that I wanted so much, and we can't even have a civil conversation. I literally want to scream at her when she spouts off."

"Maybe you should," Rick said, squeezing her shoulder lightly.

Paula lifted her head from his shoulder and looked questioningly into his face.

"I mean, she's a grown woman, but her behavior is that of a child. Maybe she wants limits; maybe she needs to know her boundaries."

"Rick, it never crossed my mind," Paula replied thoughtfully. "I feel sorry for the shape she's in, and believe me there is very little she can do for herself. I've seen the humiliation when I have to help her do the simplest of things."

"But honey, it doesn't make the things she says right or even tolerable."

Paula nodded thoughtfully.

"And don't worry about me. You are stuck with this silver-headed old man."

"Not 'old man,' middle-aged," she corrected and snuggled back into her original spot in the shelter of his shoulder. "Um, I'm going to talk to God about this. Perhaps changing my strategy is in order."

Rick chuckled and planted a kiss on her forehead.

ૐ

"Don't you have any other kind of music besides this religious junk?" Kristi complained the following morning while Paula filled the bathroom sink with warm water for her bath.

"No, ma'am," Paula replied cheerfully.

"Well, it's driving me crazy." Kristi waved her arms very dramatically.

Paula remembered her conversation with Rick. "Then turn down the intercom in your room."

"You do it; it's your house. I'm only here because I have no choice."

Paula felt a twinge of anger. "You are perfectly capable of controlling the volume on the intercom system in this room. I believe you know how to operate this wheelchair, too." She dipped a washcloth into the warm water, lathered it with soap, and handed it to Kristi. She walked out of the bathroom and proceeded to make the bed. "Beginning tomorrow you can make your own bed. There's plenty of room for your wheelchair to maneuver around both sides."

"What?" she heard Kristi ask. "I can't make my bed. Why, look at me, Mother. How can you ask such a thing?"

Paula took a deep breath before she answered. "While we are on the subject of what you can and can't do, I have a few rules to pass on."

"Rules? You've got to be kidding. I'm not a child!" she heard Kristi shout.

"Well, you certainly act like one," Paula said bravely. She bit her lip and prayed for strength. "Number one: I'm finished with your sarcasm. You are in this house because I want to help take care of you, not because I want a taste of your ugly tongue. Number two: From now on you will treat me with respect. I don't think you need a definition of the word. Number three: Rick will soon be my husband. He is to get the same respect. Number four: Stop feeling sorry for yourself. It churns my stomach and is very unbecoming. God spared you from a tragic death, and although I'd like nothing more than demand you respect Him, that has to come from you. Those four points are a good beginning. Now I'm going to pour myself a cup of coffee. When you are finished with your bath, call for me." Paula turned and left the bedroom. Kristi did not utter a word, neither did she leave her room or speak the rest of the day. Paula refused to bring a meal tray into the bedroom; Kristi knew how to get to the kitchen.

The next morning after the guests had checked out, Rick showed up unexpectedly.

"Have you bought a dress for the wedding?" he asked good-naturedly.

Paula looked at him, wishing she could see what was whirling around in his head. "Well, no, I haven't had a chance."

"Have you looked in Brenham?"

Curiosity nudged at her. "Not really. Why?"

"Why don't you go now, and I'll stay here with Kristi."

Irene laughed from behind them. "Good luck with that notion, Rick."

Paula joined in the laughter and said low, "Honey, you have no idea what you are suggesting. Then again, she hasn't spoken since yesterday. It may be pretty peaceful around here."

"I want to try," he said. "Is there anything specific you need to do for her before I run you off?"

Suddenly the idea sounded wonderful. "Yes, I need to help her bathe, but it shouldn't take long. What are you up to?"

"I'll let you know if it works."

Kristi sounded less than pleased at the prospect of spending the day with Rick Davenport.

"Can't Irene stay with me?" she demanded.

"No, Irene has things of her own to tend to. You will be perfectly fine with Rick." Kristi looked so desperate that Paula nearly gave in. "I'm going now. I'll see you when I get back."

A short time later, Rick wheeled her out into the shade and seated himself on the glider opposite her. The sky was a perfect shade of blue without a hint of clouds.

"I don't like being outside," Kristi said flatly. "It's hot and sticky and makes my casts itch."

"The fresh air will make you feel better," Rick said calmly, breathing in the midmorning breeze.

"I want to go back inside."

"Oh, I'll take you inside in a little while. I thought we'd have lunch after a bit, talk a little, and get to know each other," Rick said easily.

"I don't want to talk to you, and I certainly have no desire to eat out here with the flies and bugs." Kristi tossed her head, and the action reminded him of a little girl fixin' to throw a temper tantrum.

"Sorry, but I've made the plans," Rick said.

"Why you. . ."

"Watch what you say," he interrupted.

"Oh, are you going to tell my mother? Goodness, and I was supposed to be your baby girl."

Rick smiled, then laughed out loud. He'd just found out exactly what he suspected.

"What's so funny?" Kristi demanded.

"You, little lady. You heard your mother and I praying over

you in the hospital. That's the only way you would have known about the baby girl statement."

Kristi looked visibly flustered. Rick watched her wring her hands much like Paula did when she was upset. "So, maybe I did. It's my business."

Rick leaned over and grasped both sides of the wheelchair, commanding her attention. "Kristi, face it. You know Paula and I love you. You heard our prayers in the hospital. If I'm not mistaken, your anger and bitterness is aimed toward yourself, not your mother or me. Aren't you searching for the longing deep inside you? I think you may envy your mother's happiness and the relationship she has with Jesus Christ. I also think you want the same peace, but you're afraid. The Lord loves you, Kristi, whether you like it or not. He's calling for you to surrender to Him."

Kristi bit back the tears.

"You wanted to die in the hospital," Rick added gently. "Hitting a concrete embankment may not have been an accident."

"Stop it!" Kristi screamed. "You don't know what you're talking about!"

"You're right. I don't know the whole story. I don't know how you hurt inside, not just from the accident but deep in your soul. Only God can fill you up with His perfect peace."

"Leave me alone!" she shouted again. "Don't preach to me!"

Rick stood and hesitated before speaking again. "I'm going inside to fix us some lemonade and sandwiches. It might be a good time to do some thinking."

He watched Kristi's eyes fill with tears, and his own heart spilled over with compassion. *Oh Lord, help me with this girl. I want to help her, but I need You to guide me.*

All the while Rick prepared lunch, he kept glancing outside at Kristi, but she had her back to him. He saw her tremble and realized she must be crying. *She's crying because I hit upon some truth,* he told himself. *I hope I didn't overdo it.* He snatched up a couple of Irene's oatmeal raisin cookies and placed the food on a tray.

"Here we are," he called cheerfully. The back door slammed and Harry scurried along behind him. "You mind your manners," he said to the puppy. "None of this is for you, so sit and behave or back inside you go."

Rick pushed Kristi into the gazebo and switched on an overhead fan. With the turn of a knob, the faint sounds of a dulcimer played "What a Friend We Have in Jesus." He sat the tray in her lap, wondering and praying what to say next. He saw something strange in her hair, and he peered closer to examine it.

"Oh no," he said with a sigh. "Some nurse I am."

Red, swollen eyes lifted, confusion clearly written in her face. "What's wrong?"

"Looks like while I fixed lunch, a bird spotted you."

Kristi's eyes flew wide. "I hope you're kidding." She started to touch her hair, but instantly drew back her hand.

"Nope, I wish I was." He stood and lifted the tray from her lap. "I'll set this in the icebox until after we wash your hair."

"Wash my hair!"

Rick studied her face and a hearty laugh rose from deep within his chest. "Do you have any other suggestions?"

While Kristi leaned back in her wheelchair at the kitchen sink, Rick slipped a towel under her head and began to spray warm water into thick, dark hair. "I think I should do two soapings, don't you?" he asked.

"Yes, under the circumstances," she replied dryly, and Rick saw the embarrassment in her face. *I haven't even washed my own granddaughters' hair,* he thought amused. *I bet the two of us are a sight.*

"Your shampoo smells good, like tropical fruit. Is this other bottle a conditioner?"

"Yes," she whispered irritably.

"You don't find this funny?" he finally asked.

"Certainly not," she declared, but a slight smile rose to her lips.

Thank You, Lord, he whispered. *You sure do use the strangest things to get through to Your children.*

twenty-one

By the time Paula returned home, Kristi had elected to catch up on some reading and surprisingly enough chose the gazebo. Rick found a book in Paula's library and joined her until the sound of Paula's vehicle captured his attention.

He walked out to meet Paula, and the incident with the hair washing brought another spurt of laughter.

"Hi, honey. What's so funny?" Paula called, exiting from her truck.

"Oh the day," he said wistfully.

"Well, I prayed more than I shopped. I wanted to call so badly, but I kept my itchy fingers to myself." She pushed the lock button on her key ring. "I didn't buy a thing—saw lots of good stuff, though."

He gave her a big hug. "What a paradox. I sent you shopping and you come home empty-handed. I wonder if this will continue after we're married?"

"I doubt it," she said with a wry smile. "So, how is Kristi, or should I say how was your quality time together?" Paula asked hesitantly.

"Rather funny," he said with a chuckle. "But seriously, I found out a few things for us to pray about. Let me tell you what happened."

❧

From the sunroom window, Paula watched Rick and Kristi in the gazebo, both absorbed in their books, and yet they were together. *Oh Lord, thank You for the progress made today. I don't know how long it will take, but I know Kristi is on the right path back to You.*

An overwhelming desire to cook a special dinner propelled Paula into the pantry. She poured ingredients into a bread maker and set frozen chicken breasts to thaw in a sink of cold water.

"Um, chicken cordon bleu," she said to Tapestry. "Kristi's favorite, and I can use light cheese and ham to suit Rick's diet."

Steamed carrots and broccoli, a wild rice pilaf, and fresh fruit added to the meal. She busied herself in the kitchen and felt much happier than in previous days. She stirred together Rick's favorite light butter and herbs for the homemade bread and took another peek outside. Goodness, how she loved that man.

Allowing her mind to wander, she thought how wonderful it would be for Kristi to live with them. It didn't matter that she was a young adult. Paula only wanted her close to make up for the past five years. They could be friends, like other mother-daughter relationships, and do special things together. Maybe Kristi would feel up to shopping tomorrow when she took her to Austin for therapy. She imagined asking Kristi's opinion about the wedding dress and having lunch at a quaint tearoom. It could be so wonderful.

Paula caught herself. She realized her dreaming might cause heartache later. Desiring too much too soon from Kristi might even harm their fragile relationship. Any progress must be slow and deliberate, insuring every step of the way in the Lord's hands. If Kristi started to back off and turn inward, then Paula would have to wait. Patience and love still promised to be the best solution.

Paula and Rick expected silence from Kristi during dinner, and they were not surprised. Ignoring the young woman's unwillingness to join in conversation, they chatted on as usual.

"Mother, dinner was excellent," Kristi said at the close of the meal. She pulled her wheelchair back from the table and moved toward the kitchen counter. Paula said nothing, but she and Rick passed a smile as Kristi poured herself a cup of coffee and brought it back to the table.

"Do you mind if I look through the downstairs? I'm curious to see what you've done," Kristi sounded uncertain.

"Certainly," Paula answered. "There may be guests here

and there, but don't concern yourself about them. They're curious, too."

Kristi looked uncomfortable. "I don't want anyone to see me."

"Are you afraid they will ask questions?" Paula asked, genuinely concerned.

Kristi hesitated and took a sip of coffee. "The accident scared me to death. It's not anything I want to talk about, and I don't like people looking at me."

"Your feelings are more than understandable," Rick said, lifting his plate to carry it to the sink.

Kristi sat erect and eyed Rick squarely. "Do you always say and do the right things?" she asked sardonically.

Paula felt her heart take a dip. *No, Kristi, not now, especially when Rick's tried so hard today.*

Rick seated himself again, and Paula took the dishes from his hand. She wanted to catch his eye, but he avoided her.

"Well, you know, Kristi, I could sit here and list all my faults, but why should I? It's no secret that I'm a perfectionist, stubborn, opinionated, and bossy, but I really don't think the issue between us is about my faults or attributes, now is it?"

Kristi clucked her tongue and rolled her eyes.

"My opinionated self believes rolling your eyes at someone who has obviously irritated you expired with your sixteenth birthday." He rose from the table and poured himself a glass of ice water from the refrigerator tap.

Paula had never seen him angry—oh, exasperated at times, but not like this. His tanned face turned the shade of the fresh tomatoes on the table, and she realized the glass of water served only to calm him down.

He turned and faced Kristi squarely. "The issue at hand is power and control. With your mother single, I think you have an opportunity to manipulate her, but with her married to me, it won't be so simple. To be perfectly honest, I won't allow anyone, including myself, to manipulate Paula. Then there's the issue of the lawsuit. Have you apologized to her for that? And what about your mother's love and devotion in bringing you here to recuperate from the accident. Have you thanked her? I think not on both accounts." He set the glass on the counter and wet his lips. "I've said enough. I'm sorry, Paula."

Paula watched him walk through the kitchen and sunroom to the outside. She heard the back door shut and the sound of his boots hitting against the wooden steps. She despised controversy and instantly blamed herself for Rick's loss of control. After all, her daughter had caused the problems.

Paula toyed with the butter knife laying flat on the green checked place mat. Her own temper, rarely displayed, began to mount. Since she and Kristi first saw the farmhouse months before, Kristi had tried to undermine every decision. Paula had allowed her daughter's sarcastic tongue to spin her into an ever-circling pool of doubt and guilt. Paula felt she carried the blame for allowing it to continue.

Rick had taken time from his job and subjected himself repeatedly to Kristi's insults. He had guarded his mouth and planned his actions in hopes of winning her over. Kristi's only response was a caustic tongue.

Paula meticulously laid the silverware on top of her plate so carefully that not a chink broke the silence between herself and Kristi. For the first time since Rick left the table, she focused her eyes on her daughter. Their eyes met and a smug look swept over Kristi's face.

"Kristi, I forgive you for the years of insults and disrespect. Of course, if I had been a strong woman, I would have put a stop to it. So I ask you to forgive me for the poor parenting, because now my laziness reflects in your attitude. I love you with all my heart, but I am sincerely disappointed in you. As to what Rick said to you, I guess the truth hurts. The difference this time is that your ugly words and behavior have affected the man I love. And if you think I wasn't serious about house rules before, you'd better think again.

"I prayed for this time together while you recuperated from the accident. I hoped your hard heart would soften with the love Rick and I feel for you, but I'm at my wit's end. Perhaps I should have hired a nurse for you in Austin, because I'm fast regretting bringing you here. I don't think you want a mother;

you want a whipping boy. The sad part about it all is I've allowed it." Paula stood and looked in pity upon her daughter's impassive face. Here sat the stubborn little girl with her daddy's chin and dark eyes, her precious child all grown up and hurting. But how long should Paula allow the bitterness to affect her own life?

Paula lifted her dishes from the table. "I love you so much, Kristi, but you keep pushing me away." With those final words, she deposited her plate and silverware on the kitchen counter and walked outside in search of Rick.

She found him in the barn, grooming Floyd. Her hand touched his back, and he smiled sadly. Their eyes met briefly before he continued brushing the horse.

"I'm sorry," Paula began. "I shouldn't have forced the issue of Kristi staying here while she recuperated."

Rick shook his head. "We decided to bring her here together, and you have nothing to feel sorry about. I really thought I'd made some progress today, but instead I lost my temper. I will apologize to Kristi as soon as I cool off."

Paula picked up a curry and began working it through Boyd's mane. "Well, if it makes you feel any better, I gave her a piece of my mind. Guess I'll need to apologize, too."

"Love's hard," Rick commented. "Especially when you see someone you care about struggle with bitterness."

Paula sighed deeply and resigned herself to defeat. "I'm going to suggest she move back to Austin. She doesn't like it here, and she certainly doesn't enjoy our company."

"We probably haven't given her enough time, honey. Look, we're getting married in two weeks, and even though it's hard to admit, we both are a little stressed about the wedding. Why, you don't even have a dress yet! I'm so anxious for you to be my wife that I'm edgy and nervous."

Paula laughed. "Are you going to leave me at the altar?"

Rick peeked over top of Floyd and winked. "Not on your life, Paula Franklin, and don't you try the same thing or I'll send the Texas Rangers after you."

The next few moments were spent in silence. "How do you

feel about a walk?" Paula asked. "We can work off our tempers together and pray about what we should do next."

Rick placed his brush on a hook outside the horses' stable, and Paula followed behind him. He gathered up her hand into his and they strode across the field to their favorite spot by the creek bank.

Once The Country Charm stood in the distance, the two relaxed and began to take in the sights and sounds of the late summer evening. Paula would never grow tired of green fields dotted with pink and purple wildflowers or yellow daisies popping up along the fencerows like nature's ornaments. How could one not love the country? No city smells, no honking horns, no busyness, only beautiful, untouched meadows.

Harry had followed them and he broke the silence by yapping at a bluebird. As if on cue, insects began to sing, and it reminded Paula of the statement Jesus made when He proclaimed the rocks would cry out if His followers were not permitted to praise His name. The two walked on to the creek bank where Rick had proposed. This had become their special spot.

The cooler temperatures invited them to sit and listen, and they did so without uttering a single sound. With his arm wrapped around her and her head on his shoulder, Paula wept quietly.

"We have to believe," Rick said simply, kissing the top of her head. "Jesus loves Kristi more powerfully than we can ever imagine. We can't give up on her, honey. I feel it in my heart."

➢

By the time Rick and Paula returned to the farmhouse, Keifer had hitched up Floyd and Boyd to the wagon and assembled the guests for the nightly hayride. Inside, Kristi had disappeared into her room. Oddly enough, the table had been cleared and the kitchen looked spotless. In the middle of the table sat a plate of cookies, two mugs, and a pot of decaf coffee. The cookies were Rick's favorite, oatmeal raisin. The coffee was Paula's favorite, vanilla nut.

Together they knocked on Kristi's door to apologize and thank her for the snack. They received no response.

twenty-two

Kristi resorted to the silent treatment for the next four days. Even a trip to Austin for therapy and an exchange of the wheelchair for crutches prompted no conversation. She still hadn't toured the rest of the house and chose to stay in her room except at mealtimes. Paula talked with the pastor at the church in Brenham. His remarks confirmed Rick's views: Kristi had to make the decision to seek help and to change. No one could do it for her, and all they could do was pray.

Less than a week before the wedding, Paula realized she still hadn't a proper wedding dress.

"I've got to go into Austin and find something to wear on Sunday," Paula announced to Irene on Wednesday. "I can't believe the wedding is nearly here, and I'm not ready."

"Then go right now," Irene urged. "Maybe Barbara could help you."

Paula smiled broadly at the prospect of shopping with her old friend. "Oh, Irene, you're tempting me, but what about the work here?"

"I can manage everything. Remember who took care of things while Kristi was in the hospital?"

Paula nodded. Irene had done a fantastic job. "Yes, you handled everything magnificently. All right, I'll call Barbara and leave within the next hour." She picked up the portable phone while she headed for her bedroom. "As soon as I'm finished on the phone, I'll tell Kristi that she may be alone for a while."

"Call Mr. Rick, too," Irene reminded her.

"Thanks, I will on the car phone."

Within the hour Paula drove toward Austin, anxious to find just the right dress and to visit with Barbara. They met at the south entrance of the mall and began their search for the perfect dress or suit, according to which came first. "Ice blue or ivory," Paula said wistfully. "I wish I hadn't waited so long." The two women stared at the large selection of ladies' better wear and the formal department. The previous five stores held nothing of interest. "If we don't find anything here, let's head to a bridal shop."

The two walked through the designer fashions, even though Paula had sworn she would not spend a fortune on a dress. Both women spotted a crepe and satin ivory suit.

"That's it," Paula breathed. "Only one is left, oh tell me it's my size."

Barbara turned the tag over in her hand. "Yes!" Barbara squealed, slightly louder than she intended.

Paula lifted the suit from the rack and examined it carefully. "It's beautiful," she whispered, but when she saw the price, she immediately hung it back on the rack.

Barbara glared at her in pretended annoyance. "How much?" she asked softly.

"Four hundred dollars," Paula replied barely above a whisper.

Barbara lifted the dress and handed it to her friend. "Nonsense, buy it and wear it proudly. You have the money, and you'll only marry Rick once. I know you have a pearl necklace and earrings. All you need is shoes."

Paula grimaced. "I suppose I could try it on."

The suit hugged her trim figure as though it had been designed especially for her. The skirt fell slightly above her ankles with an appropriate slit up the left side. Ivory pearl buttons trimmed a vee neckline to the waist, and the short capped sleeves were perfect for warm weather. Paula knew she now wore her wedding dress.

More than pleased with the purchase, Paula and Barbara sat down to a delightful lunch at one of their favorite tearooms. The wedding topped their conversation. Now that all the preparations were in order, she and Rick could enjoy the next few days. They chatted away about Rick, Wade, and Kristi; but when Paula phoned her daughter, no one answered. Both women agreed Kristi was either sleeping or in one of her moods. Irene had left for a two-hour break until the guests began to arrive or Paula returned home.

Paula tried to reach Kristi again on the ride back to Brenham; again no answer. She phoned Irene and informed her that she would be at home before four o'clock and thanked her profusely for covering the bed-and-breakfast. She phoned Rick to tell him about her day, except he was busy on a construction site. They planned to meet later after dinner.

Tired and happy, Paula reached home and carried in her dress and other special purchases. She hung the ivory suit in her closet, greeted Tapestry and Harry, then headed for Kristi's bedroom. Finding it empty, she walked into the kitchen. Seeing no one there, she searched the sunroom, then opened the door to the back. Calling Kristi's name produced nothing. She could not be found.

Feeling a twinge of alarm, Paula hurried to her daughter's bedroom and glanced into the bathroom. All of Kristi's toiletries were missing. She flung open the closet door and saw that it, too, held nothing. The dresser drawers stood empty as well as the nightstand. Kristi had left The Country Charm.

*

"So what should we do?" Paula asked Rick. The two waved good-bye to the guests leaving on the hayride, hoping for a few minutes alone to discuss Kristi's disappearance. "We hadn't exchanged words since the episode at dinner, but I had no idea she planned to leave."

They walked hand in hand back to the house, each absorbed in their own thoughts about the matter.

"Honey, the question is, how do you feel about her leaving?" Rick asked.

Paula took a deep breath. "Truthfully, I'm relieved. I felt like a guest in my own house by thinking through every word and tiptoeing around her moods. I know my actions weren't right, but I was honest. Now, I'm afraid she will never work through her bitterness. Being at home in Austin provides no encouragement for her but to sink deeper into depression."

"And you feel fairly certain she went back to Austin?"

"Yes," Paula replied thoughtfully. "Kristi doesn't have close friends, and she often spoke about her condo."

"Can she legitimately take care of herself?" Rick asked. They lingered at the gazebo for a moment. The smell of honey-suckle and the faint sounds of soothing music appeared heaven-sent.

Paula nodded. "I think so, especially now with the crutches. Isn't it strange? She sued me because I couldn't take care of myself, and now we are worrying about the same thing with her. I want to try calling her at home tonight, even though I know she won't answer. If I can leave a message, perhaps she'll listen."

He played with her fingers, and Paula waited for him to speak. "I believe I'll leave a message, too. The last thing I want to be accused of is running her off. Like you, I'm concerned she will fall and not be able to get help."

"We'll have to trust God to keep her safe," Paula whispered, then she smiled. "Normally you are the one reassuring me of something. It feels good to be on the other side for a change." She looked at him with love filling her heart. "I've got to say, I had looked forward to Kristi attending the wedding, but it must not have been in His will."

Rick put his arms around her shoulders and squeezed her gently. "It may be she will more readily accept our relationship after we're married. Right now the thought of us together is a possibility, but after Sunday our union will be reality."

"Like facing the inevitable?" Paula asked thoughtfully. "Or will she shut us off forever?"

&

"This is the day the Lord has made. Let us rejoice and be glad in it," Paula said aloud. The alarm had gone off, and before the last shrill ring had sounded, her feet hit the floor.

This was her wedding day, and this was the Lord's day. Today, family and friends would join Rick and her in a beauti-ful wedding ceremony. Promptly at four o'clock, she would become Mrs. Rick Davenport. Paula hurried to the bedroom window to check on the weather. Already the sun peeked through the morning sky, and Paula knew the day promised to be perfect—even if it suddenly clouded up and rained. She grabbed her Bible and opened her devotional, but her mind kept wandering. Excitement seemed to mount through each second.

Forgive me, Lord, for not concentrating on today's devotion. I love You, and I do so thank You for today. I pray that Rick and I glorify You in every step of our life together. Be with the guests today and guard their travel. May all be blessed who share in our joy. Amen.

A twinge of sadness threatened to take hold as Paula briefly thought of Kristi. She whispered a prayer for her daughter and once more surrendered the unpleasantness between them to God. Paula shook her head to dispel the threat of gloom. She refused to allow anything to ruin this day.

She found it difficult to concentrate even on the minor tasks of preparing a country breakfast for her guests. Irene wanted to help this morning, but Paula felt her friend belonged in church with her family. She couldn't think of a single reason why she shouldn't cook breakfast for her guests. But as Paula brewed the second pot of coffee, since she forgot the grounds in the first pot, and cleaned up the broken eggs on the floor, she regretted her noble thinking. It took three trips to the upstairs sitting room to bring the coffee because she kept forgetting cream and sugar. By the time she juiced an orange and forgot to set the pitcher beneath it, her wedding jitters became hilarious.

Irene arrived in plenty of time to hear about Paula's topsy-turvy morning, then shoo her off to church. The cook reminded her that she had lots of food to prepare for a wedding in the afternoon, and too many cooks spoiled the stew. Paula laughed and gladly relinquished her apron.

At first, Paula forced herself to listen to the morning's sermon, but the topic on the many forms of love aroused her attention. After all, not everyone could worship God and get married on the same day. She didn't see Rick, but his absence didn't disturb her. Sometimes the three-year-olds in his Sunday school class delayed him for church.

Good friends wished her and Rick well and some presented gifts and cards. She suddenly wished she had planned a larger event, so all of them could share in the celebration. Paula thanked them for their generosity and hurried home. She needed to wash her hair, do her nails, see if Irene needed help, and a million other things.

It seemed strange for Rick's truck to be parked at The Country Charm, but in view of the day before them, it only served to heighten her excitement. He met her at the front door, grinning from ear to ear.

"Isn't this bad luck?" she asked, wanting to scold, but she couldn't stop smiling long enough to look serious.

He tilted his head sideways as though hearing something for the very first time. "Um, I don't remember." He reached for her, and she fell into his arms. "I love you, Paula, and this day is guarded by angels."

"Of course," she chimed. "The sun is shining, it's Sunday, and our wedding day."

"Well," he said, after planting a quick kiss upon her lips, "I have a surprise for you."

"A surprise?" she questioned. "Is not this wonderful day a surprise in itself?"

"Oh, aren't we poetic," he teased. He grabbed her hand. "Come on in."

Paula allowed Rick to usher her inside, laughing and giggling like a teenager. The aroma of a barbecue dinner tantalized her senses. "Irene, you are marvelous. The food smells heavenly." She walked into the kitchen and saw Kristi leaning over the sink with a carrot peeler in one hand and balancing on crutches.

twenty-three

Paula caught her breath. "Kristi," she breathed, and instantly all the emotions of the day surfaced to tears of joy.

Kristi turned and smiled—a smile Paula had not seen in years. "Hi, Mom! I didn't know if I was still invited, but I thought you might need a little help." Although her words were light, tears rolled down her cheeks as she spoke them.

Paula bit her lower lip to keep from crying any more, but the sight of her precious daughter gave way to another onslaught of tears. Kristi hobbled across the room without her crutches, and Paula felt too stunned to move. They reached for each other at the same time, clinging long and tight, neither willing to let go, but trying to make up for the past five years. At last Paula pulled Kristi from her own shaking body. She wiped the tears from her daughter's cheeks and swept her eyes over the young woman's face.

"I'm so sorry, Mother," Kristi said weeping. "Can you ever forgive me? I've been so horrible—just thinking about all I've done and said to you makes me so ashamed."

"Of course I forgive you, but I share in the blame, too," Paula insisted. "I wasn't such a great mother."

Kristi shook her head in protest. "You were the most fantastic mom a girl would ever want. I was simply stubborn and bitter, but things will be different now."

Paula looked at Rick and then back to Kristi. "What happened to change your mind?"

Kristi smiled sadly through her tears and pointed to Rick. "He wouldn't leave me alone. Every hour on the hour, he left messages on my machine telling me how much God loved me and how our Lord wanted me back into His arms. At the close of each message, Rick, well, I guess I can call him Dad, told me how much you and he loved me. Then he'd leave a Bible erse that always touched me in some way.

"At five o'clock this morning, he showed up at my door and old me he wasn't leaving until I came with him. He said I belonged at my mother's wedding. Goodness, I argued and called him horrible names, but he refused to take no for an answer, even when I threatened to call the police. Somehow we started talking, and for the first time he made sense to me. All of the messages he'd left suddenly sunk into my stubborn head. I agreed to breakfast and we talked about Jesus. It seemed as though my real dad sat across from me, gently persuading me to see things God's way. I saw a thousand flashbacks and another thousand times that I had been disrespectful. The pain of my own sin hurt worse than lying in the hospital and wanting to die.

"I felt like a mirror of me had been displayed in front of the whole world. Everyone could see this huge list of how I'd hurt people. When I finally prayed to confess my sin and rededicate my life to Christ, the bitterness and anger really disappeared. I wanted to see you so badly. We rushed back to the condo and I threw an outfit together and here I am."

Paula smiled through her tears. "God has made this day the happiest day of my life. I know it sounds trite, but it's true." She turned to Rick. "You have blessed my life since the first day I met you. How can I ever thank you for bringing Kristi home?"

Rick's strong arms encircled both Paula and Kristi. "By marrying me and letting me love you both. I want to pamper both of you and spoil you until you're rotten."

"No, you aren't," Kristi declared. "It's my turn. I want to make up for all the lost time. Lots of ideas are rolling around in my head, and when you two return from your honeymoon, maybe we can talk."

"Sounds good to me," Rick said, giving Kristi a squeeze. "Can't you give us a little preview?"

Kristi gave them both an ambiguous smile. "For starters, I wondered if I could stay here and help Irene while you two are gone. I'm still rather useless except for the phone, but I certainly could take reservations."

"Wonderful!" Irene shouted. She wiped her own eyes and laughed. "Cooking is my expertise, but managing The Country Charm is not."

Paula swallowed another flood of tears and thanked God for her loving family.

"My new dad gave me a tour of this beautiful house, and I'm thoroughly in love with it. Mom, you are so creative and I'm envious. Perhaps you can show me how you do it."

&

A huge yellow bumblebee tasted the nectar of the pink miniature roses in Paula's bouquet. It slowly moved from one flower to another, lingering as though it had just visited paradise. Within the arch of the gazebo, Paula and Rick waited patiently, neither wanting the other to get stung.

"It knows it's being filmed," Rick whispered with a chuckle.

The pastor had already pronounced them husband and wife, but Rick couldn't kiss his bride until the bee flew away. No one wanted to take the bouquet for fear they would taste its anger. Those standing nearby laughed at the scene and kidded Rick about sealing his commitment.

As though on cue, the huge yellow bee lifted its wings and disappeared. Paula handed the bouquet to Barbara and faced her beloved husband. The love in her face shone brighter than the September sun, and his crystal blue eyes moistened lightly as he kissed the new Mrs. Davenport.

A Letter To Our Readers

Dear Reader:

In order that we might better contribute to your reading enjoyment, we would appreciate your taking a few minutes to respond to the following questions. We welcome your comments and read each form and letter we receive. When completed, please return to the following:

Rebecca Germany, Fiction Editor
Heartsong Presents
PO Box 719
Uhrichsville, Ohio 44683

1. Did you enjoy reading *Country Charm?*
   ❑ Very much. I would like to see more books
   by this author!
   ❑ Moderately
   I would have enjoyed it more if _____
   _____
   _____

2. Are you a member of **Heartsong Presents**? Yes ❑ No❑
   If no, where did you purchase this book?_____
   _____

3. How would you rate, on a scale from 1 (poor) to 5 (superior),
   the cover design?_____

4. On a scale from 1 (poor) to 10 (superior), please rate the
   following elements.

   _____ Heroine   _____ Plot

   _____ Hero   _____ Inspirational theme

   _____ Setting   _____ Secondary characters

5. These characters were special because_____
_____
_____

6. How has this book inspired your life?_____
_____
_____

7. What settings would you like to see covered in future **Heartsong Presents** books?_____
_____
_____

8. What are some inspirational themes you would like to see treated in future books?_____
_____
_____

9. Would you be interested in reading other **Heartsong Presents** titles?   Yes ☐   No ☐

10. Please check your age range:
    ☐ Under 18   ☐ 18-24   ☐ 25-34
    ☐ 35-45   ☐ 46-55   ☐ Over 55

11. How many hours per week do you read?_____

Name _____

Occupation _____

Address _____

City _____ State _____ Zip _____

SPRING'S PROMISE

A Romantic collection of Inspirational Novellas

Experience the joy of love...

Romance readers will love this brand-new collection of contemporary inspirational novellas, all centered on the season of spring. Includes the stories *E-Love* by Gloria Brandt, *The Garden Plot* by Rebecca Germany, *Stormy Weather* by Tracie Peterson, and *Bride to Be* by Debra White Smith.

400 pages, Paperbound, 5 ³/₁₆" x 8"

❤ ❤ ❤ ❤ ❤ ❤ ❤ ❤ ❤ ❤ ❤ ❤ ❤ ❤ ❤ ❤

❤ ❤ ❤ ❤ ❤ ❤ ❤ ❤ ❤ ❤ ❤ ❤ ❤ ❤

·····Hearts♥ng·····

CONTEMPORARY ROMANCE IS CHEAPER BY THE DOZEN!

Any 12 Heartsong Presents titles for only $26.95 **

Buy any assortment of twelve Heartsong Presents **titles** and save 25% off of the already discounted price of $2.95 each!

**plus $1.00 shipping and handling per order and sales tax where applicable.

HEARTSONG PRESENTS *TITLES AVAILABLE NOW:*

(If ordering from this page, please remember to include it with the order form.)